"We haven't spoken in a couple days. Are we okay?" Nick sounded concerned.

"Why wouldn't we be?" Dani said, not feeling at all okay.

"You sure about that? You seem tense. The other night—"

"We shared a few kisses," she interrupted, proud of her nonchalant tone. "They didn't mean anything."

Only long, sleepless nights and the irritating problem of not being able to forget the feel of his lips on hers. Hot and soft...

His relieved breath was loud and clear. "That's good, because those kisses didn't mean anything to me, either. I don't want things between us to change because of them."

He had a funny way of showing it. "Me, either," Dani admitted.

During another long beat of silence, Dani racked her brain for something else to say, something to prove that she was fine.

Before she could think of anything, Nick spoke. "How about we forget those kisses ever happened."

"Consider them forgotten."

Liar, liar, pants on fire. Dani touched her lips, which even now tingled a little.

Dear Reader,

In this second book in my Prosperity, Montana miniseries, Dani Pettit is the heroine. You met Dani briefly in *A Rancher's Honor,* the first book in the miniseries. But don't worry if you haven't read it yet. This is her story, and you'll get to know her very well. Dani helps run Big Mama's Café and has high hopes of taking over the reins—if her mother retires.

Nick Kelly is a sexy rancher working hard to make his ranch profitable. Nick and Dani have been best friends since high school. They're happy as friends. But when they step over the line one night...

This is a romance you don't want to miss!

Enjoy!

Ann

I always appreciate hearing from readers. Email me at ann@annroth.net, write me c/o P.O. Box 25003, Seattle, WA 98165-1903, or visit my Ann Roth Author Facebook page. And please visit my website at www.annroth.net, sign up for my newsletter and enter the monthly drawing to win a free, autographed book! While you're there, be sure to visit the Fun Stuff page, where you'll find recipes and other fun stuff.

You can also follow @Ann_Roth on Twitter.

A RANCHER'S
REDEMPTION

—

ANN ROTH

HARLEQUIN® AMERICAN ROMANCE®

ISBN-13: 978-0-373-75541-7

A RANCHER'S REDEMPTION

Printed in U.S.A.

ABOUT THE AUTHOR

Ann Roth lives in the greater Seattle area with her husband. After earning an MBA she worked as a banker and corporate trainer. She gave up the corporate life to write, and if they awarded PhDs in writing happily-ever-after stories, she'd surely have one.

Ann loves to hear from readers. You can write her at P.O. Box 25003, Seattle, WA 98165-1903, or email her at ann@annroth.net.

Books by Ann Roth

HARLEQUIN AMERICAN ROMANCE

*Saddlers Prairie
**Prosperity, Montana

Recipe

Dani's Instant Cocoa Mix

Makes approximately 12 servings

(Note: for smaller batches, mix 2 Tbs. each of sugar and cocoa per cup of powdered milk, then add a pinch or two of salt.)

Ingredients:

3 cups instant nonfat powdered milk

6 Tbs. sugar

6 Tbs. dry, unsweetened cocoa powder

½ tsp. salt

Combine and mix thoroughly. Store in an airtight container in a cool, dry place.

To Prepare Cocoa:

Put ⅓ cup of cocoa mix in a 12-ounce mug. Stir in a little boiling water and mix until blended into a paste. Fill mug with boiling water. Stir or whip until blended. Add marshmallows if you like them.

Chapter One

Dinner was starting to smell so good that Dani Pettit's mouth watered when Nick Kelly knocked at her door. Only a few short minutes ago, she'd buzzed him into the building.

Although they talked and texted regularly, she hadn't seen him in a while. But tonight she really needed to be with her best friend.

"He's here," she told Fluff.

The tomcat meowed and trotted daintily toward the door. Which was funny because at twenty pounds and half a ton of white fur, Fluff wasn't exactly tiny. But he'd never let Dani down, and so she stifled the urge to laugh at him. There weren't many true-blue males in her life— just the cat, Nick Kelly and Dani's oldest brother, Sly. She dearly loved all three.

To prevent Fluff from darting out, running across the hall and shamelessly begging food from Mrs. Detmeier, Dani scooped him up before she opened the door and managed a smile. "Hi, Nick."

The handsome rancher flashed his pearly whites at Fluff, then gave Dani a gentler grin. "Hey."

In his large hands he cradled a bottle of wine and a white bag bearing the Lannigan's Ice Creamery logo, which was, bar none, the best ice creamery in Prosperity. Although the central Montana town of sixty thousand people boasted at least a half-dozen ice cream specialty shops, several much closer to her house than Lannigan's, Nick had chosen well. He sure knew how to brighten a girl's spirits.

Dani eyed the bag. "I hope that's rocky road."

"A whole gallon of the stuff."

"You sweetheart!" She rubbed her hands together.

Nick chuckled. "Nothing but the best for Dani Pettit."

He kissed her cheek, then set his things down to shrug out of his leather bomber jacket. He hung the jacket on the doorknob of the coat closet, just as he always did, his navy flannel shirt stretching across his strong, broad shoulders.

He was a beautiful man—tall and muscular without an ounce of extra fat, thanks to the physical demands of running a ranch. His long legs did wonders for the loose, faded jeans he favored.

Yet as gorgeous and sexy as he was, theirs was a strictly platonic relationship and always had been. Dani adored him—as a friend.

Nick stuck his fingers into Fluff's thick fur and scratched behind the cat's neck. "Howdy, Big Fella."

He refused to use the name "Fluff," which he considered too sissy for a tomcat.

Fluff didn't seem to mind. He was too busy purring and batting Nick's hand for more. A moment later, sated and content, he jumped out of Dani's arms and strolled off.

"I brought a couple of DVDs for later," Nick said. "Unless you'd rather catch a movie out. It is Saturday night."

Date night. Only twenty-four hours ago, Dani had assumed that she and Jeter would be out dancing tonight at the Bitter & Sweet Bar and Grill in downtown Prosperity, where the live music and great dance floor made the bar a happening place.

Now, dateless for the first time in three months— Dateless in Prosperity, she thought wryly—she shook her head.

After last night's painful breakup and an especially irritating day, she wanted only to relax and hang out with her best friend. "Would you mind if we stayed here? I'm not in the mood to go out."

"Staying in works."

Nick shot her a sympathetic look, and tears she refused to shed gathered behind her eyes. Jeter had never exactly treated her well, and over the months they'd been together, she'd done more than enough crying.

"I'll bet you could use a hug," Nick said. "I know I could."

Which reminded her that she wasn't the only one hurting. Earlier in the week he'd broken up with Mandy, a woman he'd seemed to really like—at least for a while. Nick had commitment issues. He claimed that he didn't want to settle down with anyone, ever, didn't want to marry or have kids. They weren't just words, either. He meant it.

Dani stepped into the warm, comforting embrace she'd needed since Jeter had dumped her. She smelled Nick's sandalwood shaving soap and fresh Montana air. And underneath both, his own "Nick" scent.

For a few long moments they held each other tightly. When they let go and stepped back, Dani felt better.

Nick sniffed the air, rubbing his belly and licking his lips, making her smile for real. "Man, that smells amazing. I've been dreaming of your mac and cheese all day."

"Even while you worked on the barn roof in the freezing rain? You're lucky it didn't snow."

It had been almost two years since Nick had repurchased Kelly Ranch, once owned by his family and then sold. Now he was slowly and painstakingly making improvements on the property, which, because it had been neglected, was rundown. His current project was the leaky barn roof. He could have hired a professional roofer, but he was watching his bank balance. Also, he claimed to enjoy doing the work himself.

"I'd prefer snow to the icy stuff we got. And yeah, I thought a lot about dinner while the sleet was pounding my head. I could eat a whole cow."

As if in agreement, his stomach growled loudly—just as the oven timer pinged, signaling the casserole was ready.

"If that isn't great timing," Dani teased. "Come on."

They linked arms and headed toward the kitchen of her little apartment, swapping fond looks with each other. "What's next on your agenda, Mr. Ranch Fixer Upper?" she asked.

"Mending fences so that we can move the livestock when the spring grass comes up. Now that it's March, that's just around the corner. I also have to install the new irrigation system soon."

"You're keeping busy, I'll give you that." Too busy to reflect much on his recent breakup. "Ever notice how you use physical labor to avoid thinking about certain things?"

He shrugged. "Hey, if it works…"

He did seem in a better frame of mind than he had when they'd talked the previous evening. "I wish I was as good at distracting myself as you," Dani said with envy.

He peered closely at her. "You've been crying."

She pulled herself to her full five-foot-six-inch height. "I was, but I'm finished now. I'm excited to spend the evening with my best friend—eating, sipping wine, having ice cream, watching a movie, eating more ice cream...."

She expected a laugh, and Nick didn't disappoint. "You and me both," he said.

While he uncorked the wine, Dani donned oven mitts and brought the casserole to her cottage-style kitchen table. "When did we last have a pity party together?" she asked as they sat down in their usual seats.

"You mean at the same time?" Nick's thick-lashed, mocha-colored eyes narrowed in thought. "I don't believe we ever have. It's usually either you or me hurting, never both of us at once."

"A first for us, then, and after sixteen years of friendship." They'd met in middle school at the age of fourteen, and had bolstered each other up through too many breakups to count.

"Bummer, huh?" Nick said. "If this is a first, we should make a toast." He filled the glasses. "To no more breakups at the same time."

"I'd rather toast to no more breakups, period," Dani said. "But I know us both too well for that."

Neither of them stayed in a relationship for long.

After setting down his glass, Nick eyed the casserole. "I'm sorry about Jeter, but I gotta say, I sure enjoy your choice of comfort food."

Dani laughed. "You always cheer me up." His sense of humor was one of his many positive qualities. "And I agree, there's nothing better than mac and cheese with hamburger." She nodded at the steaming dish. "Help yourself."

"After you." Beaming the sexy smile that made women swoon, Nick nudged the casserole her way.

He was such a gentleman, which was also sexy. "Have

you heard from Mandy since you broke up with her?" she asked when they'd both filled their plates.

"You want to talk about this now." He gave her a wary frown. "Are you trying to ruin my appetite?"

"Is that even possible? It's just that I remember how Jasmine stalked you with phone calls and texts when your relationship ended." Jasmine had been Nick's previous ex.

"She was unstable. Mandy isn't like that. We both knew we weren't going to make it."

"Too bad—she was great." Dani sighed. "What a shame she wasn't your Ms. Right."

Nick almost choked on his wine. "You're such a fairy-tale romantic. I've told you, there *is* no Ms. Right, not for me."

His track record so far certainly proved that. He never went too deep into the reasons why he found his previous girlfriends lacking, but it happened over and over. Dani suspected that his issues stemmed from his mother's extramarital affair and the subsequent breakup of his parents' marriage when he was a kid. That and the broken heart he'd suffered in his early twenties.

In all the years they'd been friends, she'd only seen Nick in love that once. He'd met Ashley in college. They'd dated for nearly a year before they graduated and moved in together. Within months of that, they were talking marriage. Then Ashley's mom, who lived in Missoula, had been diagnosed with Lou Gehrig's disease. Ashley had gone home to take care of her. She was only supposed to stay for a few months, but her relationship with Nick had fallen apart, and she never returned.

Nick claimed he'd been relieved. Even so, it had taken him ages to get over what had happened. Or maybe he never had, because he hadn't let a woman into his heart since.

Whereas Dani fell head over heels several times a year.

"And *I've* told *you* that all it takes is the right person," she said. "You can deny it until you're hoarse, but I believe that your true love and mine are out there."

"I'm not opposed to love, Dani—you know that. I just don't do it." With a shrug, he bent his head toward his plate.

"Sly used to say the same thing, and look at him now. He's happily married, with a little girl." Dani's brother and his wife, Lana, had an adorable two-and-a-half-year-old, the happy result of Lana's miracle pregnancy.

"If it can happen to Sly, it could happen to you," she went on. "And to me—I hope." She crossed her fingers and held them up.

Nick failed to comment.

"Out of all the women in the world, one is perfect for you," she said. "Someday when you meet her, you'll see."

"Trust me, between the available women in Prosperity and the summer tourists who come through every year, I'm a happy man."

"Except before, during and after the breakups." She bit her lip. "I did everything I could to make Jeter love me as much as I loved him. What's wrong with me?"

Nick shook his head. "That's the wrong question. You should be asking, *what's wrong with Jeter?* You've got to quit trying to please the guys you date and be yourself. You're great just as you are."

Nick had always been wonderful at boosting her self-esteem. "You're sweet," she said.

"I mean it, Dani. Now, about the guys you date. You say you want to get married and have a family, but you pick guys who don't. Guys like me." He shook his head. "Most of them are jerks, too. That's why you get hurt."

"So you and Sly keep pointing out." Dani fiddled with her napkin. "I guess I'll take a little break from dating."

"That's probably a wise idea."

Except that she hated sitting home alone on a Saturday night. "I'll make plans to go out with some of my girlfriends instead." But that posed a problem, because at the moment, most of them were either in a relationship or married. "That is, if I can find someone who's free to get together on a Saturday night."

"I'm available," Nick said. "You can hang with me."

"Until your next girlfriend comes along."

"That could be a while."

"Ha." Dani hated being single. Maybe her plan to take a break from dating had been made too hastily. She let out a heavy sigh.

Nick gave her a measured look. "You're already wishing you had another guy in the wings, aren't you? Just do me a favor. The next time you date someone, hold on to your heart until you're sure he's worthy enough to give it to."

"And just how do I do that?"

He stroked his strong chin pensively. "It might help if you try going out with a different kind of guy than your usual type. Someone who isn't a bum."

He was right, most of the males Dani dated were pretty much jerks. As she sipped her wine, she thought about why she made such poor choices. There was nothing more attractive than a good-looking man with a spark of wild in his eyes and a devil-may-care attitude. She'd certainly fallen for enough of them.

And where had that gotten her? Every new relationship started out filled with promise, making her ever hopeful that this time, this boyfriend would love her and treat her right. And although she tried everything to make him happy, from wearing clothes he liked to embracing the activities he enjoyed—even when she didn't—sooner or later things always soured.

Nick just might have a point. She sat up straight. "You're right—I should try dating someone I wouldn't normally choose. Drumroll please. When I do decide to date again, I'll pick a man I wouldn't usually look twice at."

Nick frowned. "Define a man you 'wouldn't normally choose.'"

"Well, someone hard-working, with both feet on the ground. And he has to have a good job." That way, he wouldn't ask to borrow money from her, as Jeter had. "If he's impatient about getting physical and refuses to move slowly, he's out."

"Having a regular job doesn't make a man a decent human being," Nick said. "At first, guys tend to put their best foot forward. How can you tell the square shooters from the jerks until you get to know them?"

"Hmm." Propping her chin on her fist, Dani pondered the question. "Well, I'll do what you said, and hold my heart in check for a while. And maybe, instead of waiting for the man to ask me out, I'll do the asking. I'll start by observing him for a while when he isn't looking, and I'll pay attention to how he treats other people. That'll give me a glimmer of an idea of his character."

Nick gave an approving nod. "That's not a bad plan. It's definitely worth a try."

Dani smiled. "So glad you approve, Mr. Kelly."

AFTER THREE HELPINGS of mac and cheese, Nick's belly was satisfied. He and Dani lingered at the table, both of them relaxed. He was also too beat to move. Fixing up the ranch and making it profitable was an all-consuming job, filled with unexpected obstacles and on-going challenges. Not that he minded. He loved his land. But with another full day starting at oh-dark-thirty tomorrow, he was ready to head home and fall into a dreamless sleep. Dani appeared to be just as tired.

"Are you sure you want to watch a movie tonight?" he asked after she yawned for the second time. "You have to get up even earlier than I do, and with Big Mama riding your case…."

"Don't remind me." Dani grimaced. "Ever since the Poplar Tree restaurant opened and the *Prosperity Daily News* ran that story about them, business at the café has been slipping. How many times have I told Big Mama that we need to step things up and make some changes in order to compete? Does she listen? Heck, no."

Everyone who knew Trudy Alexander called her Big Mama. The nickname suited the five-foot-eleven, two-hundred-plus-pound female. Although she towered an intimidating five inches over Dani, Dani gave her as good as she got. They were both strong-willed women, and they often butted heads. And yet, their love for each other was obvious.

At the tender age of four Dani had lost her mother to cancer. Two years later she'd also lost her father, when a tree limb had crashed through the windshield of his car, killing him instantly. The freak accident had left Dani and her two older brothers orphans. The boys had been taken in by an uncle in Iowa. He hadn't wanted a girl, and Dani had gone into Prosperity's foster care system. Luckily for her, she'd been placed with Big Mama. A couple years later, the older woman had legally adopted Dani, with Dani keeping her original last name.

"I know our customers," Dani went on. "I should—I'm there six days a week, from five o'clock in the morning until we close at 2:00 p.m., and often for a few hours after that. I waitress, I order food and supplies, help with the hiring and firing, and I sort the mail. Most of those are responsibilities I've handled since I was in high school. The only things I don't do are the cooking and the financial stuff."

"You work hard," Nick agreed. As hard as he did, for which he respected her.

"And I do a good job—a really good job. So why doesn't Big Mama trust me to make decisions that could help our restaurant?" Dani snickered. "Heck, she doesn't even trust me to get through a Saturday or Sunday without nagging me about one thing or another."

Presumably Dani's mom, now in her late sixties, would retire someday and Dani would take over. But handing the reins over to anyone, even her daughter, wasn't proving easy for her. For now, Big Mama preferred to run the business her own way, keeping Dani on a tight leash. Nick had been hearing about it from Dani for several years now. "Of course she trusts you," he said. "She just prefers to be in control."

"If she trusted me she wouldn't *have* to be in control. You wouldn't believe the day I had, much of it courtesy of her." Dani grimaced again. "Which is a long way of answering your question. No, I don't want to call it a night just yet. I'm so ready to escape into a movie, and I want to do it with my best friend."

As bone-tired as Nick was, Dani needed him and he wasn't going to let her down. She and Big Mama were like family to him. He was a lot closer to them than to his own sister and mother. Dani was loyal to the people she cared about. Even when she was in a bad relationship, she stayed true to her boyfriend. His fickle mom, on the other hand, didn't know the meaning of loyalty.

"Today was worse than usual?" he asked.

"It was pretty bad."

"What happened?"

Dani slanted her head. "Are you sure you want to hear about this?"

If talking about her day took her mind off Jeter, Nick was all for it. "Sure."

"How long have I been running the restaurant on weekends so that Big Mama can take a few days off?" Dani grumbled. "As if she's ever really 'off.' Business has slacked a little lately, but that doesn't mean I stand around, twiddling my thumbs. She must've called ten times today, making sure I'd done this chore and that one. Have I cleaned the tables and reset them after customers finished and left? Have I checked the salt-and-pepper shakers and the sugar bowls to make sure they're filled? You'd think I was a new hire. I just wish she'd get that I know what I'm doing and let me do it."

She didn't expect a comment, so Nick just nodded.

"I've done tons of research on steps we could take to increase our business," she continued. "But no, she finds something wrong with every one of my ideas. I even suggested she watch *Restaurant: Impossible,* the Food Network show about saving restaurants from going under, so that she could see what other restaurants are trying. She claims she doesn't have time for that."

Dani's lips pursed in irritation. She was definitely in a tough situation.

"Maybe I can help," Nick offered. "Big Mama's crazy about me." She always had been. As a teenager, he'd spent more nights at her dinner table than his own mother's. "Let me talk to her."

"No, thanks. I'll handle this myself. Besides, she's so

stubborn that not even your Kelly charm could budge her on this. It's enough that you're letting me whine."

Dani had always been an independent female—except when it came to men. She fell in love fast, and tried way too hard to please whoever she was with.

Nick didn't do love, period. What was the point of falling for a woman when love would ruin a man's life? Because sooner or later, the relationship was bound to end. Women were fickle and not to be trusted—Dani excepted.

"Big Mama started her business forty years ago," he said. "Anyone would have difficulty letting go."

"And I get that, but it doesn't make my working life any easier. I want her to trust me, Nick." Dani *needed* her mother's trust. Owning and running a restaurant wasn't easy, and Big Mama wasn't getting any younger. She deserved to retire and let Dani take over. "Okay, I'm through complaining—for now." She switched gears. "Let's watch a movie so that I can forget about work and Jeter."

"Soon," Nick said. "But first, ice cream with hot fudge sauce, if you have any. Let's eat in front of the tube."

Her eyes lit up. They were an unusual silvery-blue, the same color as Sly's and those of their brother, Seth, whom Nick had met a few times when he and Dani had first become friends. But then Seth had left town, and Dani and Sly hadn't seen or heard from him in years. They had no idea where he was.

"I like the way you think, Mr. Kelly. And yes, I happen to have bought a fresh jar of hot fudge sauce on my way home today—just for you."

Nick had been to her apartment so often, he knew where she stored everything. In the pine cabinet to the right of the sink, he found the bowls. The drawer next to the stove yielded the ice cream scoop. Dani opened the jar of fudge sauce and heated it in the microwave. By the time he piled ice cream into the bowls the fudge sauce was nice and hot.

"I want first crack at that sauce," Dani said with a teasing twinkle in her eyes. "Otherwise, you'll eat the whole thing."

Nick gave her a look of mock hurt. "I'd never do that."

"Ha. Your sweet tooth is so big that mine dims by comparison. But you never gain an ounce, you lucky man." She sighed. "I wish I could eat whatever I wanted and not put on weight. That's the one good thing about my breakup with Jeter. I won't have to diet anymore."

Jeter had ridden Dani's case about her weight but Nick thought he was nuts. "What do you care about some Neanderthal's opinion?" he said. "You're perfect the way you are."

And she was. Curvy in all the right places. With pretty eyes and a plump mouth made for kissing, she could attract any man she wanted. Plus, she was warm and friendly, with a heart as big as the Montana sky.

Nick was crazy about her, but not in a sexual sense. As attractive as Dani was, he considered her a cross between sister and best friend. That was the whole reason they'd stayed close all these years. Sex would just mess up their relationship.

Dani finished drizzling a stream of hot fudge sauce over her rocky road. "Have at it." She handed Nick the jar of sauce, but kept the chocolate-coated spoon for herself.

After slathering his ice cream with enough chocolate to satisfy his sweet tooth, he stuck his finger in the jar and scraped it clean.

Dani laughed. "Sure you got enough?"

Her smile was contagious, and Nick grinned. "For now. Let's go watch a movie."

They headed for the living room. "What DVDs did you bring?" Dani asked.

"Only the first two James Bond movies ever made— *Dr. No* and *From Russia with Love*."

"James Bond?" She stuck out her lower lip. "Come on, Nick, my heart is broken. You know that when I'm sad my preference is for three-hanky love stories." She brightened. "I haven't watched *The Holiday* since last Christmas. I could put it on."

Nick had seen the chick flick with her so many times he'd memorized most of the lines. He made a face. "After every one of your breakups, we watch movies that make you cry. You've cried too much over Jeter."

Within weeks after they'd started dating, Jeter had hurt her by sticking her with their dinner tab at a restaurant and taking off with his friends. Nick had wanted to deck the loser and teach him some manners, but that would have infuriated Dani. Instead, he'd encouraged her to quit trying to make the bum happy when he wasn't doing a thing to make *her* happy. He'd also suggested she break off with him. But she'd already been in love and Nick's words had fallen on deaf ears. It was a relief to know that next time she'd choose a different kind of man.

"Why don't we mix it up and try a spy film. How about it?" He tugged on a lock of her pretty brown hair, which she wore straight and almost to her shoulders, then picked up the two DVDs. "Trust me, either of these classic Bond flicks will take your mind completely off your broken heart and your bad day. But hey, if you'd rather cry instead and waste another box of tissues…"

"You're right." She squared her shoulders. "Okay, I'll

give *Dr. No* a try. But if I can't get into it, we switch to *The Holiday.* Deal?"

"Fair enough."

Dessert in hand, they shoved the four colorful throw pillows—Dani was big into bright colors—to one end of the couch and then sat down.

Looking hopefully at Dani's bowl, the ridiculously named Fluff jumped up between her and Nick. "No," she said in a stern voice. "The vet put you on a diet, remember? Besides, this stuff is bad for you." She shooed the cat away.

Undaunted, he jumped onto the floor and then butted Nick's shin, his yellow eyes pleading. Nick was unmoved. "You heard the lady. This sundae is all mine."

Tail high, the offended tom stalked off.

Nick slid *Dr. No* into the DVD player, then dug into his sundae. With any luck the combination of the sugar jolt and the action would keep him awake for a few hours.

Within moments Dani was totally engrossed in the film to the point that her ice cream melted. It was obvious she wasn't thinking about Jeter or the restaurant now.

Mission accomplished. Nick smiled to himself.

He watched the film for a while, but not long after he finished his sundae, his eyelids grew too heavy to stay open. He set the bowl on the coffee table. It was the last thing he remembered.

Chapter Two

Dani opened her eyes. As entertaining and exciting as *Dr. No* was—and it was so dated that it was both—she'd fallen asleep in the middle of the action. Now she was snuggled against Nick's side, with her head on his chest. His arms were wrapped around her, holding her close.

When had that happened?

By the steady rise and fall of his rib cage, he'd also fallen asleep. Poor guy was exhausted, and yet he'd come over tonight so that they could cheer each other up. Although he'd done most of the cheerleading.

Tenderness flooded her. She loved him dearly, but cuddling with him stretched the bonds of their platonic relationship.

Doing her best not to disturb him, she gently began to untangle herself from his grasp. Not so easy, as he was holding on tight. Without meaning to, she woke him. His sleepy, sexy smile stole her breath. She was marveling at the power of that smile when he lowered his head and kissed her. On the mouth. He'd never done that before.

As startled as Dani was, she liked the solid feel of his arms anchoring her close. Liked his lips brushing warmly over hers. Dear God in heaven, he could kiss. Without knowing how it happened, she melted into his hard body and kissed him back.

He tasted of chocolate and ice cream and something subtle that she recognized as uniquely him. His big palms slid up her sides, dangerously close to her suddenly tingling breasts.

Okay, this was getting out of hand. Dani stiffened and pushed him away. "Don't, Nick."

"Jeezus." He released her as if she'd burned him. "What are we doing?"

She touched her lips with her fingers, noting that his gaze followed and settled on her mouth.

"I'm not sure," she said. "All I know is that sometime during the movie we both fell asleep. And then—"

"We were making out. Wow." Nick scrubbed his hand over his face. "Sorry about that."

Dani should be, too. Only she wasn't.

No wonder the women Nick dated went nuts over him. Not only was he sexy and funny with good manners, he also knew how to kiss. Fan-yourself-go-soft-inside kisses that emptied the mind of all common sense.

Dani sensed that he could also do a lot of other equally wonderful things with his mouth. Blushing furiously, she leaned forward and stacked their bowls.

She almost wished...

But no. Nick was exactly the kind of guy she'd just sworn off of, a man who moved from woman to woman and kept his heart under close guard. Besides, he was her best friend. His friendship was important to her, and she wouldn't do anything to jeopardize it.

Nick lifted the dishes right out of her hands, then stood. "It's late, and tomorrow will be a long day for both of us. I should go," he said, taking the words straight from her kiss-addled brain.

Dani wanted him to leave so that she could recover from a colossal mistake. She also rose. While Nick deposited the bowls in the kitchen, she fluffed the throw pillows and repositioned them along the couch.

When he returned, he shrugged into his jacket, which only accentuated his flat belly and broad shoulders.

"I'll, uh, talk to you later." He grabbed hold of the doorknob as if he couldn't get out of her apartment fast enough.

Normally when they parted he kissed her on the cheek. Now that she was tingly and hot everywhere, even the most chaste kiss would be dangerous.

Fluff came running. Why couldn't he have fallen asleep between them and prevented what had happened? Dani scooped him up and held him to her chest like a shield, poor cat. She opened the door and stood well out of reach until Nick moved through it and strode rapidly down the hall, away from her. After shutting the door, she let Fluff down. She didn't draw in a normal breath until she heard the elevator close behind Nick.

NICK WAS UP at the crack of dawn Monday morning, relishing the busy day ahead. After a hearty breakfast he pulled on wool socks and entered the mudroom, where he tugged on boots and donned a heavy jacket. He stepped onto the back porch, his breath puffing from his lips like smoke. It was a cloudy March morning and chilly, but not quite cold enough to snow. Instead, heavy rain was predicted. Not the best working conditions for installing an irrigation system.

As always, the sight of the rolling fields filled him with pride and made him think of his father, a man who had died way too soon. Nick Senior had taught Nick that land was the most important thing a man could own, but his actions had jeopardized everything.

Kelly Ranch had belonged to the family for generations, until Nick's parents had fallen on hard times—thanks partly to the vagaries of Montana weather, but mostly because of his father's lavish spending habits. Nick remembered the jewelry, fancy appliances and high-end new car his father had bought his mother. He'd been so wrapped up in keeping her in luxury that he'd neglected the ranch. Neglect that had cost them all in the worst way possible.

Before long, unable to keep up with the mortgage and credit card debt, the family had been forced to sell. Nick's parents had moved with him and his older sister, Jamie, to the east side of Prosperity. The poor side of town.

Both his parents had soon found jobs that paid regularly and provided a much-needed steady income that helped stave off the bill collectors. But no one had liked living in the city. Nick's parents had fought constantly, and his mother started working late. She'd taken up with a man at work, someone else's husband. The affair had ended, but not before it destroyed both marriages and broke up two families.

Breathing in the crisp air, Nick started down the back steps. He'd always wondered what his life would have been like if his parents had managed their debt better and had held on to the ranch. Would they have stayed together? If they had, his life would have been totally different.

But playing the what-if game was an endless circle of unanswerables. Nick didn't want to remember that time, or the bitterness that had clung to his father like a shroud afterward and until the day he'd died.

He headed across the yard toward the shed where he stored tractors and other large ranching equipment, the cold earth crunching under his boots. The only positive thing to come out of his dad's untimely death was the insurance policy he'd left Nick. Thanks to that unexpected gift, Nick had suddenly had the funds for a down payment on the family ranch, which had just happened to be on the market. It was rundown and had come dirt-cheap, and he'd been able to put down a decent amount. Using what remained of his inheritance, he was slowly making much-needed improvements.

Unfortunately, the cost of the new irrigation would eat up the last of the money. And there was so much yet to do before Kelly Ranch finally turned a profit. Several outbuildings still required repairs, and the ranch needed a new hay baler. Nick also wanted to add more cattle to his herd. While those things would have to wait, Nick was proud of the fact that the ranch should be fully restored and profitable within in the next two years—as long as he kept his eye on his goal. He wouldn't slip up like his father, who'd lost everything. All for a woman who'd ended up leaving him, anyway.

At least the land was back in the family, where it belonged.

From the direction of the trailers that housed his ranch crew, a rooster crowed as if in approval. Nick had three permanent ranch hands. Two were married, and their wives raised chickens.

With an eye to cutting costs, he'd commandeered two of the men to help with the grunt work on the irrigation system.

They were waiting for him at the shed. Nick nodded at Palmer, the foreman who'd agreed to stay on when he'd bought the ranch, and Clip, a brawny twenty-five-year-old who wasn't afraid of hard work. Jerome, the third member of the crew, was tackling the regular chores today.

"Morning," he greeted them. "Kenny Tripp, the irrigation specialist I hired to install our new system, should be here soon."

While they waited, they stood around, sipping coffee from thermoses and talking about their weekends.

"Hey, how's Dani doing?" Clip asked.

She occasionally visited the ranch, and the crew knew that Nick had gone to her place Saturday evening, to console her after her breakup.

Unsure how to best answer Clip's question, and preferring not to discuss about what had happened between him and Dani, Nick took a long pull on his coffee. He wasn't often confused by his own actions, but kissing her...

What the hell had gotten into him?

Yeah, he'd been half-asleep when it happened, but that was no excuse. Over the years they'd fallen asleep beside each other plenty of times without him ever making a move on her. She meant too much to him to wreck their relationship by getting physical.

But then, he'd never guessed that kissing her would be so mind-numbingly powerful or that she'd get under his skin the way she had. The feel of her lips under his, the sweet press of her breasts against his chest...

"She's doing okay," he said gruffly.

He drained the last of his mug, screwed the cap on the thermos and gave himself a mental kick in the butt. Dani was his best friend. Kissing her or anything beyond that was off-limits. He'd had no business pulling her as close as he could, and no business wanting to strip her naked and get even closer.

At the mere thought, his body tightened. Turning away from Palmer's narrow-eyed scrutiny, he set his empty thermos on a shelf near the door. Tonight he would call Dani and assure her he wouldn't be crossing the line with her ever again.

Clip grinned. "Now that she's single again, I just might ask her out."

The bachelor cowboy was full of himself.

Nick gave him a warning look. "I wouldn't."

"Why not? She's available."

"Because she deserves a man who'll stick around and build a life with her."

"Heck, I'll stick to her." Clip chuckled at his joke until Nick glared at him. The cowboy sobered right up. "Chill out, Nick, I'm only funnin' around."

The sound of a truck rumbling toward the shed drew Nick's attention. "That must be Tripp now. Let's go."

He opened the door and Palmer and Clip followed him out.

On Mondays, Big Mama's Café was closed. As much as Dani loved going in to work, a day off was always a welcome relief. A chance to relax, read the newspaper from cover to cover and sleep in....

Scratch sleeping in. She'd been getting up before dawn since high school, and the habit was hard to break. Plus, she had a lot on her mind, first and foremost the meeting at Big Mama's house this morning. Her mother didn't handle change well, but today, Dani was determined to persuade her that making needed alterations was critical to the restaurant's survival.

The very thought of that conversation gave her hives.

Then there was Fluff, who expected his breakfast no later than five-thirty. Sitting on her chest, all twenty pounds of him, he batted her chin with his paw and meowed. Loudly and plaintively. "Oh, all right, Mr. Alarm Clock," she muttered, moving him aside so that she could flip on the reading lamp on the beside table. Yawning and stretching, she fell back against the pillow again.

She'd spent a long, restless night, and not just because she was stressing over the upcoming conversation with Big Mama. Nick Kelly had played a big roll in the tossing and turning.

They didn't get together all that often, but they touched base frequently, either by phone, text or email. But since Saturday night, Nick hadn't called or texted her once. Dani hadn't contacted him, either. Their friendship was hugely important to her, and she hoped those unforgettable kisses hadn't made things between them all wonky.

Key word: *unforgettable.* A man didn't kiss a woman as thoroughly as Nick had kissed her without making a huge impact. And what an impact it had been. Dani wanted more of the same. A lot more.

Which was just too bad, because she wasn't about to kiss Nick like that again. Ever. The smartest thing to do was to forget the other night had ever happened.

Fluff amped up his cries to earsplitting level. "Will you stop?" she snapped in a sharp tone that caused the cat to grow quiet.

He fixed her with an accusing look that caused an instant case of the guilts. None of this was his fault.

Gentling her voice, she rubbed behind his head. He promptly forgave her and began to purr. What a pushover. "You're such a sweet boy," she crooned. "Let me stop in the bathroom on my way to the kitchen. Then I'll feed you."

By the time she threw on a robe and padded into the kitchen a few minutes later, the cat was pacing anxiously in front of his food dish. Her heart went out to him. Roughly two years ago she'd adopted him from a cat shelter, not long after he'd been found abandoned and starving. He still worried about his food, and if she didn't feed him first thing in the morning, he tended to get upset.

Dani needed coffee, but it would have to wait. "You know how I am before my morning dose of caffeine," she said. "But just this once, I'll give you breakfast before I put the coffee on." She filled his bowl. "There you go. This just proves how much I care about you."

Busy scarfing down his meal, Fluff ignored her. Wasn't that just like a male? Once you gave him what he wanted, he didn't spare you a second thought.

"Story of my life," she murmured.

Twenty minutes later she felt human again. Sipping her second cup of coffee, she read most of the *Prosperity Daily News* instead of skimming it, an indulgence she had time for only on Mondays.

After a leisurely shower she dressed in jeans and a pullover sweater, then grabbed her purse and a coat, and blew the cat a kiss. "Bye, handsome. Behave yourself while I'm gone."

When she pulled out of her parking space in the apartment complex, ominous clouds filled the sky. Dani groaned. Not more rain.

Big Mama lived in the same two-story bungalow where Dani had grown up. When she arrived at the house some ten minutes later, rain was coming down hard and the wipers were working overtime.

Jewel Sellers's old Lincoln Continental was parked behind Big Mama's SUV, which was in the carport. Jewel was her mother's best friend and they often palled around. Dani hoped the woman wasn't planning on staying. She and her mom were supposed to talk about the restaurant.

She parked beside the Lincoln. At the Pattersons' house next door, Gumbo, a ten-year-old mixed chow female, dashed down the steps from the covered porch, barking a hello. The Pattersons were both at work, and Gumbo was obviously lonesome.

Dani pulled the hood on her coat over her head and stopped at the chain-link fence. Hunkering down, she stuck her fingers through to pat the wet dog, who she swore grinned at her despite the driving rain. "Hey there, Gumbo. You should stay up on the porch, where it's dry."

Ignoring her advice, the dog licked her fingers. "Aw, I love you, too," Dani said. "I wish I could stay and visit with you, but it's too wet and cold. Besides, Big Mama's expecting me. When Jewel leaves, we're having a 'meeting.'" She pantomimed sticking her thumb down her throat, then lowered her voice. "If you can figure out a way to make Big Mama accept even *some* of my ideas and trust me enough to quit micromanaging me on weekends, I'd love to hear them. There'll be a doggie treat in it for you. Gotta run now."

She raced up the steps of the covered porch. The front door was unlocked, and once she removed her wet shoes and shook the rain water from her coat, she let herself in. After the damp cold outside, the house felt snug and dry. The familiar aromas of lemon oil furniture polish and freshly baked treats that smelled out of this world flooded her nostrils. Salivating, she hung her coat in the closet.

"Hey, it's me," she called out, just as she always had.

Her mother bustled in from the kitchen, her gait a little slower than it once had been, but still brisk. Dressed in her trademark off-white blouse and dark pants, bifocals propped on her head, she greeted Dani with a warm smile.

Jewel followed, as petite and trim as Big Mama was large.

"I was hoping to see you before I left." Jewel tsked in sympathy. "I'm sorry about your breakup."

"Thanks." It was no surprise that she'd heard about that. Big Mama kept her well-informed. Still, Dani wasn't about to discuss the details. "It's nasty out there, so be careful," she said.

Her mother peered out the little window in the door. "What a storm we're having. The weather people are warning about a three-dayer. Lordy, I hope they're wrong. Be safe, Jewel. I'll see you Friday night."

The woman nodded. "Six o'clock, dinner out and cards here." She patted her large handbag. "Thanks for the cinnamon roll. It will go well with my afternoon coffee. You're in for a yummy snack, Dani."

When the door closed behind her, Dani's mother opened her arms. "How about a hug for your Big Mama?"

Dani stepped into the familiar embrace. Instantly she was enveloped in Big Mama's warmth and lilac cologne, and for a few seconds all her cares faded. For all their disagreements, Dani loved her dearly.

"What was Jewel doing here?" she asked when they let go of each other.

"You know what early birds we both are. She's going to knit me a cardigan and wanted to show me possible yarns and colors."

"That's nice," Dani said. "I hope you picked something with a little color." Not that her mother wore colors much. Everything she owned was either black, brown or navy.

"I did—a soft gray. You hungry?"

Having skipped breakfast, Dani nodded. "Those cinnamon rolls smell wonderful."

"Of course they do." Big Mama grinned. "I took a batch out of the oven just before you got here. I left the nuts out, the way you prefer them. There's a pot of hot coffee, too."

Eager to eat something, and always up for another cup of coffee, Dani rubbed her hands together. Then she frowned. "Didn't Dr. Adelson tell you to cut down on fats and sweets?"

Her mother made a face. "I don't smoke and I don't drink. Isn't that enough? Besides, what's the point of living if I can't indulge in a few of the things I love?" With a defiant gleam in her eye, she raised her chin. "A treat now and then won't hurt."

Before Dani could argue, Big Mama changed the subject. "You have circles under your eyes." She scrutinized Dani critically and pursed her lips. "You're not sleeping well. It's because of Jeter, isn't it? I didn't want to ask and bother you while you were at work this weekend, but how are you doing?"

Bother her? She'd only driven Dani crazy with her frequent calls. Dani refrained from pointing this out. She had more important things to discuss. "I stayed up late last night, but that had nothing to do with the breakup," she explained. "I'm actually doing okay."

"You're already over Jeter?"

Nick's kisses had all but wiped the other man from her mind. *Kisses I'm going to forget,* she reminded herself. "Pretty much."

"That was fast—much faster than usual. Let's get at those cinnamon rolls while they're still hot. Spending Saturday evening with Nick must've done you a world of good," Big Mama said as they sauntered toward the kitchen. "I just adore that boy."

Nick was no boy—he was all man. Fighting the urge to glance away from her mother's shrewd blue eyes,

Dani shrugged. "I guess I wasn't that in love with Jeter, after all."

"I'm relieved. He wasn't the one for you. What did you and Nick do to cheer each other up?"

Although the rain had changed into pounding hail, Dani suddenly wished she was outside. Anything would be better than answering that question. "We had dinner and talked. And we ate hot fudge sundaes," she said. All of which was true. "Then we watched an old James Bond movie called *Dr. No.*"

"I remember that movie. Ursula Andress co-starred with Sean Connery."

The scarred old oak table that had been around since Dani's childhood was set for two, with a couple of jumbo cinnamon rolls on each plate. More than Dani could ever eat. The promised pot of steaming coffee and a pitcher of warm milk sat beside a stick of creamery butter and a vase of pussy willow buds. Ancient furniture and dishes that weren't all that different from those at Big Mama's Café—battle-worn, but friendly and homey. The food both here and at the restaurant was always excellent, but it was also very rich. People loved eating it, but these days they also needed other, healthier options.

Pushing that conversation aside for now, Dani sat in her customary seat, facing the window that overlooked the backyard where she'd spent many a happy spring and summer day. The curtains were open to let in the gray light. Hail bounced like white BB's against the concrete patio.

Seemingly oblivious to the spectacle, Big Mama sighed as she buttered a roll. "Sean Connery—now there's a man. He's still as handsome as ever."

For a long moment neither of them spoke, other than to exclaim over the flaky cinnamon rolls. Dani thought back to when she was six and Big Mama first took her in. At the time her then foster mother had been forty-five and widowed for almost four years.

Big Mama married late in life, and she and Winston had been madly in love. They'd been husband and wife just over a year when Big Mama had learned she was pregnant. She and Winston were ecstatic.

Then one snowy night her husband had died in a twenty-car pile-up on the freeway. A few weeks later, Big Mama miscarried. After that, she'd lost her interest in men, and had spent her days running the restaurant and raising Dani.

"I made a decision I'm sure you'll approve of," Dani said. "From now on, I'm going to date only the kind of man who has a steady job. He should also want to get married and have kids."

Big Mama nodded. "That's smart, Dani. But I want you to consider something important—you don't need a man to be happy."

Her mother had never said this before. Dani stared at her. "Hey, I happen to *like* men."

"They are wonderful, but after I lost Winston, I did all right by myself. Especially when it came to you. When you were growing up, we sure had a lot of fun." She waited for Dani's nod, then continued. "I may not have given birth to you, but I raised you as my own, and I did it totally without help. And I did a darned fine job of it, if I do say so. You became a terrific young woman. I'm so proud of you."

Dani flushed with pleasure. "Aww, thanks."

Big Mama had saved her from what could have been a childhood as awful as the one that Sly and Seth, her brothers, had endured at the hands of a distant uncle. Uncle George had taken them in but hadn't wanted Dani.

At first, that had hurt, but his rejection had turned out to be the best thing for her. Because Uncle George disliked kids—even his own nephews. Poor Sly and Seth had borne the brunt of his animosity.

Whereas for Dani, from the start Big Mama had made her feel welcome and comfortable. She'd taught Dani how to cook and had let her help out in the restaurant. She'd always treated her with kindness and respect—along with a strong dose of discipline. By the age of eight, Dani had become the woman's adopted daughter, in every way possible. She'd soon inherited Big Mama's love of feeding hungry diners delicious, homemade food, along with the desire to manage a well-run establishment that brought people back again and again.

That wasn't happening so much anymore, but if Dani could just make the changes she wanted, she was sure that business would pick up. "I'm forever grateful for you and the wonderful life you've given me," she said. "But I'd still like to have a husband and a baby or two. Don't you want a grandchild to spoil?"

"Of course I would, but what I want most for you is your happiness."

With her mother in such an expansive mood, this seemed the perfect moment to get down to business. Tamping down a bad case of nerves, Dani reached for her purse and pulled out a folder. "I put together a couple of new menu ideas that will appeal to health-conscious eaters, as well as an updated look for our menu." The restaurant's interior hadn't changed since Dani had first stepped inside it some twenty-four years ago. It was now dated and not exactly welcoming. In fact, the drab decor and old lighting contradicted what Dani considered important—not only delicious food, but a bright, fun atmosphere in which to enjoy it.

She pointed to the crude sketch she'd made. "I'm no artist, but you get the gist. This design is more contemporary and will suit the new decor perfectly."

Her mother didn't bother to put on her bifocals. "Just hold on there, missy." Her lips thinned into a stubborn line. "I haven't agreed to any new decor. And we don't need new menus or recipes, either. We have great food and friendly service, and customers like us just the way we are."

Here we go. Dani stifled a sigh. "You're right, but there's a lot of competition out there now, and we're steadily losing business, especially since the Poplar Tree opened. If we want to keep the customers we have and attract new ones, we have to make changes and update the restaurant."

An emotion that Dani swore was fear crossed her mother's face, gone so quickly that she wondered if she'd imagined it.

"Not on my watch," her mother stated firmly.

Dani suppressed a groan of frustration. The restaurant was to be her legacy, and she wanted it to survive and flourish for the rest of her life and even longer. "I'm only suggesting these things because I care about the restaurant as much as you do," she said in what she considered a reasonable tone.

Her mother stiffened and folded her meaty arms over her chest.

Okay, then. "What do you suggest we do instead?" Dani said, oh, so genially.

Big Mama *humphed*—so much for going the polite route. "We won't do anything. Big Mama's Café will remain as it always has been. We serve the best breakfasts and lunches in town. If people don't believe that, then they *should* eat someplace else."

Why couldn't her mother see that the atmosphere and menu made them look out of step compared to other restaurants? "You are so darned stubborn!" Dani fumed.

"I don't want to talk about this anymore." Her mother's jaw clamped shut.

Once again she'd failed to convince her mother to make any changes. Dani threw up her hands. Back to the drawing board.

Chapter Three

By Monday evening the hail had changed into sleet. Wondering whether it would snow, Dani sat on her living room floor with Fluff at her side, listening to a Josh Turner album and getting ready to fold the laundry she'd washed this afternoon. She loved the masculine sound of the country singer's voice.

Nick's voice was deep and sexy, too…

She frowned. She still hadn't heard from him, which was upsetting. Before Saturday night, she'd have picked up the phone and called him without a thought. But now, it just didn't feel right.

Between his silence and Big Mama's refusal to make a single change to the restaurant, Dani was frustrated enough to scream. Plucking one of the throw pillows from the couch, she covered her face to muffle the sound and let loose with a loud scream. Several of them.

When she removed the pillow from her face, she was in a better mood. Fluff had darted under the couch, but with a little patience and coaxing, he came out.

Dani went back to folding her clean things.

From the time she'd first come to live with Big Mama, her job had been to sort and fold the clean laundry. The task of transforming a rumpled basket of freshly dried clothing into smooth, neat piles had always relaxed her. Tonight she needed to relax and clear her mind.

No worrying about the restaurant, Big Mama or Nick. Just her and Josh Turner, singing together.

The basket was half empty and Dani was belting along to "Would You Go With Me" and in a much better place, when her cell phone rang. She checked the screen—Nick. Finally. Her heart bumped joyously in her chest.

She tamped down that happy feeling and focused on being annoyed. After lowering the volume of the music she picked up the call. "Hi, Nick," she said, not bothering to warm up her tone.

"Uh…" A brief pause. "Am I catching you at a bad time?"

"Not really. I'm folding laundry."

"That should make you nice and relaxed."

She had been, until now.

When she didn't comment, Nick went on. "We haven't spoken in a couple days. Are we okay?"

"Why wouldn't we be?" she said, not at all okay.

Fluff chose that moment to jump into the laundry basket. Soon his long hair would be all over her clean clothes. Dani lifted up the cat and set him on the carpet. After narrowing his eyes at her he flounced off with his tail high.

"You sure about that? You seem tense. The other night—"

"We shared a few kisses," she interrupted, proud of her nonchalant tone. "They didn't mean anything."

Only long, sleepless nights and the irritating problem of not being able to forget the feel of his lips on hers. Hot and soft…

His relieved breath was loud and clear. "That's good,

because those kisses didn't mean anything to me, either. I don't want things between us to change because of them."

He had a funny way of showing it. "Me, either," Dani admitted. "Why did it take you so long to call?"

"You didn't pick up the phone and call me, either."

"I guess I needed time to process what happened."

"Ditto."

During another long beat of silence, Dani racked her brain for something else to say, something to prove that she was fine.

Before she could drum up anything, Nick spoke. "How about we forget those kisses ever happened?"

"Consider them forgotten."

Liar, liar, pants on fire. Dani touched her lips, which even now tingled a little.

"You and Big Mama had that meeting at her place today. How'd it go?"

The great—and occasionally annoying—thing about Nick was that he remembered most everything she told him. "Don't remind me," she said, frustrated with her mother all over again. "I don't know why I thought she'd listen this time. I came prepared, too, with a sketch for the new menu. I even brought recipe ideas. Big Mama gave everything a thumbs-down, so I asked for *her* ideas. She had nothing to say, except that she won't make a single change. She just keeps repeating that both our food and service are excellent just as they are."

"They *are* important."

"Of course. But the same old, same old isn't enough anymore—not if we want to stay in business. We both want the restaurant to thrive again. Why won't she try something new?"

"Maybe she's scared."

"My mother?" Dani snorted. "Of what?"

"I don't know—spending the money?"

"Since she refuses to give me access to our financial information, I have no idea. All I know is that we can't afford *not* to change."

Sharing her worries with Nick helped, and as Dani talked, her anger at him melted away. Yet now, a different kind of tension simmered between them, the kind that made her self-conscious and a little ill-at-ease.

"I'm not asking her to totally gut the place, though in my opinion, that would be the best option," she went on. "But new tables, chairs, curtains and wall decorations, better lighting, fresh paint and an updated menu? That'll cost a bit, but not that much. There has to be a way to convince her, but heck if I have a clue what it is."

"My offer still stands," he said. "I can talk to her."

"No, it's best if you stay out of this. I'll handle it myself. How was your day?"

"It's your battle—got it. My day sucked. This crappy weather delayed the irrigation project. Tripp and his team won't be back until the rain eases off."

"That's too bad. When the team finally does start, how long will the whole thing take?"

"Tripp estimates about five days."

"To irrigate the entire ranch? That's not bad."

"Nope, and during the dry days of summer, I'll be glad I did it. My mom called this afternoon."

"No kidding," Dani said. Nick and his mother weren't close, but she and Dani got along okay. "It's been ages since you heard from her. What did she want?"

"She asked me to come over after work Friday."

Dani was puzzled. "I wonder why."

"If I know my mother, she needs money."

He sounded disgusted. Despite having a job that paid

decently, his mother always seemed short of cash. And she often borrowed from Nick to make up the gap.

"Are you going?" Dani asked.

"If I don't, she'll nag me until I do."

There the conversation died.

They usually chatted easily about everything under the sun, but tonight Dani couldn't think of anything else to say. Apparently neither could Nick.

The ensuing silence was uncomfortable.

Finally Nick cleared his throat. "You probably want to get back to your laundry and then to bed. I'll let you go. Sweet dreams."

His signature sign-off. Tonight, Dani wasn't sure what kinds of dreams she'd have. She hoped they didn't feature Nick doing delicious things to her… "You, too," she said. "Good luck with your mom."

They both disconnected.

Feeling oddly discombobulated, she folded the rest of the laundry and wondered how long it would take before she and Nick were at ease with each other again.

AFTER TWO DAYS of torrential rain and intermittent hail, the downpour suddenly braked to a stop just as darkness hit. During the nasty weather Nick, Palmer, Clip and Jerome had spent much of their waking hours fighting to keep the swelling river at the north end of the ranch from flooding the surrounding pastures. Meanwhile Blake and Wally, two seasonal ranch hands in need of work, had offered to herd the cattle to dry ground. The two men had impressed Nick, and he'd offered them jobs to last through September.

Now hungry, muddy and wet, he showered and put on a clean flannel shirt and jeans. After phoning in an order for a jumbo pie with the works he jumped in the truck and headed for Harper's Pizza, his favorite.

As usual, the small pizza hut was packed. Salivating over the mouth-watering aroma of the pizzas, Nick nodded at people he knew and shared flood stories with several ranchers before taking his place in the crowd waiting near the takeout window. Every few minutes the teenage kid manning the window called out some lucky Joe's name to pick up their order.

In the midst of the noise, the door opened and a redhead sauntered inside. Nick wasn't the only guy who checked her out. Flashing a pretty smile, she joined him in line.

"What a big crowd tonight," she commented. "The bad weather must've kept people home for a few days, and I guess they're making up for lost time."

Nick nodded. "It's been a heck of a few days."

"My hair and I are both relieved that it finally stopped raining." With an apologetic smile, she touched her hair. "It gets crazy wild."

"Curly looks good on you," Nick said. So did the long sweater she wore in place of a coat. A wide leather belt emphasized her small waist and rounded hips. She had long legs, too. Pretty face, nice body—just his type.

For some reason he flashed on Dani and the redhot kisses they'd shared the other night. But Dani was off-limits. They were friends, period, and they'd both agreed to forget those kisses had ever happened. "I'm Nick Kelly," he said.

"Hello, Nick Kelly." The woman tossed her head, drawing his attention to her slender neck and a pair of long, dangly earrings. "I'm Sylvie Kitchen."

They shook hands. Sylvie's fingers were slender and warm. Attraction flared in her eyes.

Nick waited for a similar spark, but felt only mild interest. Maybe if he got to know her a little better...

During the ten minutes they waited for their pizzas he learned that she worked for the local tourism department, which after ranching, was the second biggest business in Prosperity. During the late spring and early summer months, hiking, camping and bicycling swelled the town by as much as ten thousand people.

"To kick off this year's tourist season, we're going to host a joint function with Prosperity Park," she said. The park housed Prosperity Falls, an eye-popping cascading waterfall that was a popular place for marriage proposals and outdoor weddings and drew visitors from all over. "It's going to take place in mid-April. I could get a couple of tickets for you and your girlfriend."

"I don't have a girlfriend right now," he said.

"Oh?" She flashed a pleased smile. "Maybe you'll want to bring someone."

She arched her eyebrow and angled her chin slightly, as if half expecting him to ask her out.

"Nick Kelly, your order's ready," the teenage boy called out.

Nick signaled that he'd be right there, then redirected his attention to Sylvie. "I'd like to, but spring is pretty busy at the ranch. I doubt I'll be able to make it."

She seemed genuinely disappointed. "Here's my card," she said, scribbling something on the back. "If you change your mind, give me a call."

Before slipping the card into his pocket he glanced at what she'd written. *In case you want to reach me after hours,* and a number.

Minutes later, shaking his head, he carried the pizza to his truck. A beautiful woman had just given him her number, but he didn't want to call her.

What was wrong with him?

DANI LIKED EVERYTHING about Pettit Ranch—the vastness of her brother's holdings, the hints of new spring grass coloring in the brown winter pastures, the grazing horses and cattle everywhere you looked. Most of all, the home Sly shared with his wife, Lana, and their daughter. Tonight Sly had gone to Tim Carpenter's ranch, which was five hundred or so acres down the road, for a spur-of-the-moment Thursday poker game. Lana had invited Dani over for a girls' evening.

"I come bearing gifts," she said when Lana opened the front door. "Chinese, from Chung's." A take-out place they both loved. "And chocolate chip cookies, courtesy of Big Mama's Café."

"I so love those cookies!" Lana looked grateful, as well as tired. Between running two successful daycares and being mom to Johanna, a spunky two-and-a-half-year-old, she had her hands full.

As soon as Dani stepped through the door, the little girl squealed and threw herself at her knees.

"Hi, pumpkin!" Laughing, Dani scooped her up and swung her around.

Johanna giggled and held out her arms for more. "Again, Dani!"

She was no lightweight, but Dani couldn't resist her adorableness. She spun around twice more, each time with Johanna reaching out to her and begging, "Again!"

Finally, breathless and worn out, Dani quit. "That was fun, but I'm pooped, Johanna. Now I want to visit with Mommy."

Sometime later, she and Lana lingered over the dwindling pile of chocolate chip cookies, while Johanna marched around the kitchen, pounding on an old pan with a wooden spoon.

"She's so cute," Dani said.

"The cutest two-and-a-half year old ever, but then, I'm biased." Lana laughed. "Sly and I are getting baby-hungry again." She glanced at her daughter and lowered her voice. "Yesterday we signed up with an adoption agency. Of course, another miracle could happen. We could get pregnant again. But that's unlikely, and we want another child."

"I'll keep my fingers crossed," Dani said.

Drawn by their soft voices, Johanna stopped at the table. Her eyes lit on the cookies. "I want a cookie, Mama."

"How do you ask?" Lana said.

"Please."

"May I share some of mine with her?" Dani asked.

Lana nodded. "A small piece."

Carefully breaking off a tiny chunk of her cookie, Dani gave it to her niece.

"Thank you." The happy little girl kissed Dani's cheek, then stuffed the treat into her mouth and continued marching around the kitchen.

"She adores you," Lana pointed out. "And you're so wonderful with her. Someday you're going to make such a great mom."

"First, I need to meet a guy who actually wants to settle down and start a family."

"You will."

"With my track record?"

"You forget that I'd basically given up on love when I met Sly. And look at me now." Lana gave a dreamy smile. She and Sly had been married for two-plus years and they still acted like love-sick honeymooners. Dani envied them.

Her traitorous mind went straight to the one man she

was trying *not* to think about—Nick. "Things have gotten weird with Nick," she confided.

Lana frowned. "How so?"

"Swear you won't tell Sly." Dani's oldest brother, who was seven years older than she was, tended to be on the protective side.

"I promise." All ears, Lana leaned forward.

Assured, Dani explained. "You remember that Nick came over Saturday night."

Lana nodded. "So that you could keep each other company after your breakups. I've always admired how you support each other that way."

"Right. We had our usual great time together, but when we were watching a DVD after dinner, we fell asleep together on the couch. When I woke up, we were snuggled up close." Remembering Dani hugged herself. "When Nick woke up, we kissed."

"Is that all?" Lana waved her hand dismissively. "There's nothing wrong with a kiss between friends."

"This wasn't exactly a friendly peck," Dani said. "Nick and I... We've always had an unwritten rule—we might buss each other on the cheek, but never on the lips. But those kisses..."

Talking about it was like reliving the experience. Dani's lips and entire body warmed right up. She fanned herself.

"*Those* kisses? As in more than one?" Lana's eyebrows jumped upward.

"A lot more." Dani let out a sigh. "We made out, Lana."

"You and Nick *made out?*" her sister-in-law repeated, sounding incredulous.

"Guilty as charged."

"And you enjoyed it."

Dani nodded miserably. "That would be a definite yes."

"Wow." Lana shook her head slowly and wonderingly. "I always sensed that you two were attracted to each other. How could you not be? He's gorgeous, you're gorgeous… What took you so long to figure it out?"

Dani knew she wasn't half bad. She also know she was far from gorgeous. She gaped at Lana. "What are you talking about? Before Saturday night, there *was* no physical attraction between Nick and me." Or if there had been, they'd hidden it from themselves and each other. "We don't want a physical relationship. Our friendship means too much to us."

"That shouldn't be a problem. Friendship and passion are essentials for a solid relationship. Look at Sly and me. He has my back and I have his, and I consider him to be one of my best friends. And we're definitely not platonic. At all." Lana's smile oozed sexual satisfaction.

As much as Dani loved her sister-in-law, she sometimes wanted to hate her for living the life she'd always wanted. "You know how it is with me, though," she said. "Some guy gives me a sexy smile and a few decent kisses, and I'm half in love. Once we have sex, I'm a total goner. But Nick…he doesn't do love."

Lana gave her a skeptical look. "A lot of guys say that, but then they meet the right woman and bam! They're all in."

"Not Nick. He's so against falling in love that as soon as he starts to fall for someone, he ends the relationship. Trust me, I know. Getting physical would spell disaster for our friendship. We've been best friends forever, and neither of us want to lose what we have now. That's why we can't cross over the boundaries of friendship."

"Let me get this straight—you and Nick both agree that a physical relationship could jeopardize your friendship. If you're on the same page, how is that a problem?" Lana frowned.

"You wouldn't think we'd have one, would you?" Dani said. "But since Saturday night, things have gotten a little tense between us."

"Ah. So…despite what you just said about not wanting to cross the arbitrary boundaries you two have established, you and Nick aren't quite on the same page anymore."

"But we are," Dani argued. "We both agreed to forget we ever kissed."

Lana gave a wry smile. "And how's that working out for you?"

Dani rested her head on her fist. "For me, not so well. I have no idea about Nick, except that when we last spoke on the phone, it was awkward. That was Monday. We haven't been in touch with each other since."

Three whole days—an eternity.

"I wouldn't worry too much," Lana said. "Our weather has been awful. Until last night, Sly and his guys were putting in twenty-hour days, with barely a moment to eat or sleep. That's why he's playing poker tonight—to give himself a well-deserved break from the ranch. I'll bet Nick has been just as busy."

"Probably. Still, he could've called last night, just to check in. Or at the very least, texted. That's what he's done in the past."

"And you're wondering if he's staying away because of those kisses."

"A little."

Lana bit her lip in sympathy, making Dani feel even worse. "What do you want to do?" she asked.

"I'm not going to call him," Dani said. "I'm keeping busy. Which reminds me. I don't have any plans Saturday night. If you and Sly want a date night, I'm happy to come over and babysit."

"That's sweet, but my parents have already offered. They're hosting an overnight for Johanna and her cousins. Johanna is excited. So are Sly and I. We'll get a whole night to ourselves." Lana all but salivated. "Didn't you and a couple of girlfriends sign up for a silk painting class Saturday afternoon? Why don't you hang out with them afterward? Go to dinner and out dancing, or catch a movie, or shop."

The idea appealed to Dani. "I'm pretty sure Christy and her fiancé have plans, but Becca and Janelle might be free. By the way, I have a new dating plan," she said, her own words filling her with hope. "From now on, I'm going to go out with a different kind of guy. He'll have a decent job and be looking to settle down and get married."

Once she met her Mr. Right, she'd be able to forget all about Nick's kisses. Then they could return to being just friends.

Lana opened her mouth to say something, but Johanna broke into noisy tears and barreled into her mother's arms.

"What's the matter, sweetie?" she asked, pulling the howling toddler onto her lap.

"Owie," Johanna wailed, pointing to a red place on her kneecap.

"Aww, poor Johanna. Let Mama make it better." Lana placed a tender kiss on the injury.

Instantly, the cries turned into sniffles. "C-can I have a Band-Aid?"

"It'll come right off in the bathtub, but why not? Dani, will you grab the box of Tinker Bell strips from the bathroom cabinet?"

Moments later, Lana kissed her daughter's cheek. "Is that better?"

Johanna studied her bandaged knee and nodded.

"This has been fun, but Johanna needs a bath before bed," Lana said. "Then we're both going to sleep."

"I need to get to bed myself," Dani said.

After pulling on her coat and kissing her niece and sister-in-law, she opened the door.

"Good luck with your dating plan," Lana said. "Keep me posted."

Chapter Four

"Hey, Mom," Nick said when his mother let him into her apartment late Friday afternoon.

At five feet three, she was short enough that he had to bend down to kiss her cheek.

He nodded to his sister, Jamie, who was two years older than him and sitting on the couch, idly thumbing through a magazine. "Didn't expect to see you here."

She shrugged. "When Mom says to show up, I do."

They'd both been divorced twice, and were as tight as a mother and daughter could be.

Nick narrowed his eyes at his mother. "What's this about?"

"Does there have to be a reason for me to want the company of both my son and my daughter?" she asked. "I've missed you, Nick. It's been too long."

"Since the last time you asked for money." She'd never been shy about asking him for a loan. Since his father had left him the insurance policy, the requests had only increased.

She put on her pouting face. "That's mean."

"It's the truth."

His mother didn't deny it. "For your information, I happen to have news I want to share in person."

Magazine forgotten, Jamie sat up straight and gave her mother a canny smile. "Is this about Dave?"

Dave, the fiftysomething manager of their mother's apartment complex, had been hanging around for years. Smiling like a cat who'd just snagged a bird for dinner, his mother nodded.

"He finally popped the question." Without waiting for an answer, Jamie squealed, jumped up and hugged her mother.

Nick's mother squealed, too. When they let go of each other, she held out her hand, showing off her newest engagement ring. Dave had always seemed a frugal man, but by the sheer size of the diamond, he'd spent a hefty chunk of change.

It was even bigger than the ring Nick's dad had bought for his mom not long before they'd sold the ranch.

Dave was a nice guy—a couple rungs up from his mom's previous husband. That marriage had been doomed from the start and had failed after less than two years. Nick just hoped that if, by some miracle, this one lasted, she didn't reduce Dave to the broke and unhappy man his father had become.

"Congratulations," he said, wondering why she hadn't just called with the news. "How much do you need for the wedding?"

She actually seemed offended. "I don't want your money, Nick," she said, surprising him.

He figured that after how much the ring had probably set Dave back, the man probably didn't have anything left.

"Dave and I have decided to keep things simple and private," he mother said. "We'll get married by a justice of the peace, either in late April or early May. I want you both to come."

"The spring market is the last weekend in April," Nick reminded her. Proceeds from the sale of his stock at that market paid the ranch expenses for the rest of the year. He couldn't miss it.

"Then how about the first Friday in May?"

Nick and Jamie exchanged glances.

Nick shrugged. "Works for me."

"I'll ask for the afternoon off," Jamie said. She did hair and makeup at a swishy salon. "Should be fine. I can't wait to do your hair and nails, Mom."

They squealed again.

"Jamie, if you want to invite Hank, he's welcome." Her current boyfriend. "Nick, you should bring Dani."

"Dani," he said, wondering at that. "Why would you want her to be there?"

"Girlfriends come and go, but Dani will always a part of your life. I like her. She balances you out."

Not understanding, he frowned.

"When she's around, you're happier and more relaxed than when she isn't."

Not so much anymore.

"You two are such close friends and she and I have known each other for such a long time, that I'm sure she'll want to come," she added.

In the past, a comment about his closeness to her wouldn't have bothered him. It did now, and that rattled him more than the words themselves.

"I'll ask her," he said.

"You know I'd hang out with you tonight if I didn't have a date," Dani's friend Janelle said as they stood in the parking lot of the art studio after their silk painting class.

It was dusk, and they'd spent the past four hours painting silk scarves that they could actually wear. Dani had enjoyed herself, painting, laughing and creating along with her friends. The instructor wanted to set the colors on the scarves so that they didn't bleed, and had promised to mail the finished products to each of them the following week.

"Ditto what Janelle said," Becca said. "Let's plan to go out together some other Saturday night."

As disappointed as Dani was, she understood. Just now, she regretted that she was taking a break from dating. On the other hand, this was a good opportunity to prove to Big Mama that she could be perfectly happy without a man.

All she needed was something fun to do tonight.

"I'm available," Christy said. She'd been unusually quiet all afternoon, but had seemed to enjoy the art class as much as the rest of them.

Dani's jaw dropped. In just over five months, at the end of August, Christy was getting married to her boyfriend, Per. He'd proposed last Christmas. Now they were sharing an apartment. Saturday nights, they always lined up something fun to do together. "Are you sure? I mean, you and Per usually have plans."

"I could use a girls' night out." Christy's lower lip quivered and her eyes filled.

She tended to be a drama queen, but who could ignore a statement like that? About to go their separate ways, Janelle and Becca stopped, exchanged looks with Dani, and drew closer.

"What's wrong, Christy?" Dani asked.

"If I talk about it, I'll cry."

"Like none of us has ever cried in front of you." Dani patted her large shoulder bag. "I have tissues."

Christy glanced around the parking lot, where a few women from art class lingered. "Not here."

"There's a coffee place a few blocks away," Becca said. "Let's go there."

Christy hesitated. "Don't you have to get ready for your date?"

"We're not going out until nine."

"Don is picking me up at eight," Janelle said. "That's two hours from now."

The coffeehouse, a renovated one-story bungalow, was filled with all things cowboy—lassos, Stetsons and photos of young, handsome men, some galloping across the prairie on powerful horses, others herding cattle or roping steer. Each man was attractive, but none could compare with Nick. They probably couldn't kiss half as well, either.

Dani pushed the delicious memory of those kisses right out of her head. She wasn't going to think of Nick that way.

At just after six, the café was getting ready to close and was almost deserted. As soon as they sat down with their coffees, Christy started talking.

"I've dreamed of getting married at Prosperity Falls since I was a little girl," she said, twisting her sparkly, half-carat engagement ring around her finger.

Didn't everyone? Couples from all over the area got engaged and married within sight of the beautiful falls.

"You couldn't book the date you wanted," Dani guessed, stifling the urge to roll her eyes. This was typical Christy drama.

"Actually, I was able to schedule exactly the time and date I wanted," her friend replied.

"Okay." Becca's puzzled expression echoed Dani's own. "So what's the problem?"

"The problem is that Per wants to elope and then host a big party for our family and friends." Christy let out an indignant huff. "Elope? Is he kidding? No way! A girl only gets married once in a lifetime—at least, I hope so—and I want everyone to witness our joy and commitment!"

Every sentence was a shriek, and the few people still in the coffeehouse were staring.

"Why would he want to elope?" Janelle asked.

"To save money so that we can buy a house sooner."

A big saver herself—Big Mama had taught her the value of putting away money for a rainy day—Dani nodded. "That's not a bad idea. It's nice and practical."

Christy gave her a *whose side are you on?* frown. "A wedding is no time for practicalities. I want a big one, and I'm going to have it. I'm the bride, and it's my right."

She seemed so unhappy that Dani had to ask. "Are you having second thoughts about marrying Per?"

"No! Yes. I don't know." Christy pushed her barely touched mug away.

Becca and Janelle seemed worried now, as worried as Dani. If Per and Christy weren't solid, who was?

Christy's phone rang. She actually jumped. Clearly she was wound as tight as a spring. "That's him now. Excuse me." She stood and hurried out of the coffeehouse.

"I hope they work things out," Dani said.

"They will because they love each other." Becca stirred what was left of her cappuccino. "Of course she wants to marry Per. I've always been jealous of how much he loves her. He would do anything for her. I want a man like that."

"Me, too." Dani sighed. If only she could stop fantasizing about Nick....

"It's too bad you and Nick don't want to get together."

Since when had Becca become a mind reader? Dani gave her a wide-eyed stare. "You know exactly why."

After swearing them to secrecy earlier, she'd told them what had happened.

"Because Nick's similar to the guys you usually date—out for some fun, then buh-bye." Becca shrugged.

"And because you'd rather stay friends than be lovers and lose it all later," Janelle added. "Also, you have that new dating plan."

Dani laughed. "At least you both listened."

"But he invited you to his mom's wedding," Becca said.

Last night, Nick had called for that very reason, another awkward conversation that had ended quickly. "That's not for almost two months, and a justice of the peace is marrying them," Dani reminded her.

Although the entire ceremony wouldn't take more than fifteen minutes, Dani was nervous about attending. Before those kisses she was trying so hard to forget—BK, for short—she wouldn't have thought twice about attending his mom's third wedding. But now... From the words the couple would exchange to the rings they would slip on each others' fingers, it was bound to be awkward.

"Nick doesn't even want to go," she said. "He only invited me because his mom asked him to."

"You make it sound as if he's taking you to watch a root canal," Janelle commented.

With things so tense between them, it felt a little like that.

They were on their second cups of coffee when Christy finally rejoined them.

"I can't go out with you tonight, after all," she told Dani, her expression and body language worlds lighter than they had been before Per's call. "I'm going home to Per so that we can work things out."

Dani and her friends breathed collective sighs of relief.

In the parking lot they shared a group hug and then went their separate ways.

In no mood to go home and spend Saturday night brooding about her problems, Dani vowed to create her own fun. She drove to Second Time Around, a movie theater across town that played second-run movies and old classics.

Tonight's double header was a two-for-one Ladies' Classic Night, featuring *Moonstruck* and *An Officer and A Gentleman*. The romance, the funny moments, the tears, the happy endings—Dani loved everything about both movies. The theater was almost full, with mostly women and older couples. After buying herself a soft drink and a large, buttered popcorn—tonight's dinner— she found an empty seat in the last row and settled in.

She sat through both movies, nibbling popcorn and sipping soda, while alternately laughing and bawling her eyes out. First for Loretta and Ronny, and later for Paula and Zack.

When the house lights came on, the popcorn and soda were gone and Dani felt very sorry for herself. Forget creating her own fun—she wanted a love like that of the couples in the movies. Like Christy and Per's.

Refusing to attend a pity party for one, she pasted a smile on her face as she left the theater. "I'm a strong person, and I'm going to be okay," she assured herself.

Then and there, she decided to start acting on her dating plan sooner rather than later. So what if she'd been single for only a week? She was ready to climb back in the saddle.

And this time she would approach dating in a smarter way. She wouldn't let herself fall in love until she was absolutely certain that whoever she dated was a steady, solid man who wanted to settle down, get married and have kids.

She considered calling Nick and alerting him that she was going to put her dating plan into action sooner rather than later, or maybe stopping by and explaining in person. But it was after eleven on a Saturday night. She needed to get to bed, and anyway, he was probably out. Besides, the way things were between them, she couldn't just pick up the phone or stop by. She would tell him when they next talked.

On the way home, she detoured to Lannigan's to cheer herself up with a double cup of rocky road, caramel sauce and whipped cream. But scant minutes before she arrived, the ice creamery closed for the night. Shoot, she wouldn't get what she wanted, after all.

Didn't that just sum up her life lately? Pathetic.

In a blue funk despite her resolve to stay strong, she headed for home. "Tomorrow's a new day," she assured herself.

Sunday was the last day of her work week. That was something to be happy about. Soon, she would start searching for someone to date. The right man for her was out there, she just knew it.

Already she felt better.

SATURDAY NIGHT, NICK headed for Tommy's, a bar with beer on tap and great spicy chicken wings. When he arrived, Ted and Paul, two buds from college, already had a table and a pitcher.

Ted, an engineer, was wearing his trademark red St. Louis Cards baseball cap and grinning as if he'd just been drafted as the team's first baseman. "Hey, Nick."

Nick nodded and sat down at the table. "What's with him?" he asked Paul.

Sporting a goatee and a sour expression, Paul, who managed commercial property for a big company, snickered. "Beats me. He's been wearing that dopey grin since he got here. Odds are, it has something to do with Marcie." Ted's wife. "Guy's been married for eighteen months, and for some reason he still acts like he's on his honeymoon. Crazy fool."

Paul had been divorced almost six years and was still nursing a grudge. His failure to move on reminded Nick of his father, who hadn't let go of his anger at Nick's mother until he was on his deathbed. Nick didn't blame his old man for being pissed off—he'd been just as mad at her for breaking up the family. But holding on to that anger hadn't done his father any good, and Nick was pretty sure all that bitterness had contributed to the heart attack that had killed him. At the same time, his father's desperation to please his mother had cost him the ranch. Nick didn't ever plan on being bitter or wrapped around some woman's finger that way. Making the ranch profitable was his main focus, and he wasn't about to ever let any female get under his skin and distract him. It was best to play the field and keep his sanity intact.

He poured himself a beer. "Spill it, Ted."

Instead of speaking, the man handed out cigars.

"What's this?" Nick frowned. "We don't smoke, and we sure as hell can't light up in here."

"They're symbolic—to celebrate something really huge," Ted explained. "Marcie and I are expecting."

Grinning, Nick fist-bumped him. "Congrats, man."

Ted beamed. "We're excited."

"Hey, that's great, but did you and Marcie want kids this soon?" Paul said.

"We'd planned to wait another year or so, but it's all good. Our baby's due in October."

"Is it a boy or a girl?" Nick asked. Dani would want to know—when he told her. Over the past week, they'd only spoken twice, and both times had been a struggle.

"Can't say for sure," Ted said. "We're holding out for a girl, but we won't find out the baby's sex for a couple months yet."

"That's our waitress up at the bar." Paul stood. "I'll order the jumbo plate of chicken wings, fries and another pitcher."

"What's eating him?" Nick asked as Paul strode toward the bar.

"You remember that promotion he was up for? He got passed over."

Nick didn't comment and neither did Ted, but they both understood that Paul's bad attitude was partly to blame.

"How are things at the ranch?" Ted asked.

"We're halfway through installing an irrigation system." Nick brought his friend up to speed on his plans, before moving on. "My mom's getting married again."

"For the third time?" Ted shook his head. "Maybe this will be the charm. You happy about that?"

Nick hadn't thought much about it. He'd been too worried about bringing Dani with him to the ceremony. Given the tension between them, he wasn't sure he should, even if his mother wanted him to. He shrugged. "Dave's all right."

Paul returned to the table. "The order's in, and another pitcher is coming. Hey, Nick, there's a woman over there who reminds me of Dani." He nodded across the way.

Half hoping it *was* Dani, Nick craned his neck around, where a brown-haired woman in jeans and a T-shirt was sitting with a group of men and women.

Besides being at least a decade older than Dani, she

was nowhere near as pretty. "She's nothing like Dani," he said.

"Must be the way she wears her hair," Paul said. "Speaking of Dani, how's she doing?"

Nick wasn't sure. He hoped she wasn't sitting at home tonight, with nothing on the calendar. "She's getting over a breakup, but doing okay," he said.

Paul's eyes narrowed in a probing look. "Are you?"

Wondering if his friend somehow sensed that things had shifted between him and Dani, Nick narrowed his eyes. "What's that supposed to mean?"

Unphased, Nick's buddy grinned. "I was talking about *your* breakup. So Dani's okay and you're crappy. I'm getting an interesting picture here."

Just then the waitress showed up with a fresh pitcher, saving Nick from God only knew what else Paul might say. He didn't want to think about what had happened with Dani. Or talk about it. He wasn't that kind of guy.

He filled his plate and shifted the subject to basketball and March Madness, which started in less than two weeks.

To his relief, Dani's name didn't come up again.

Chapter Five

The next week, Charlie Schorr, a customer who'd become a Friday breakfast regular since moving to town some six months earlier, greeted Dani with his usual smile and held out a white carnation. "Good morning, pretty lady. This is for you."

Built like a linebacker, single and about ten years older than she was, he wasn't bad-looking. He didn't float her boat, but he'd been flirting with her since the first morning he'd sat down in her station. Lately he'd taken to bringing her a flower every Friday, which was sweet. He tipped generously, too.

"Aw, thanks, Charlie." She placed the flower in the small vase that sat on the corner of the hostess desk, for all to enjoy.

Wearing a pleased smile, Charlie sauntered to his favorite booth.

He seemed nice and had a job as a CPA. And bonus: he was single. At first glance, he was exactly the kind of man she'd vowed to date—even if she wasn't attracted to him.

But that no longer mattered. She had a new plan and was keen to test it out. Couldn't hurt to give Charlie a chance.

Dani didn't know his thoughts on marriage and kids,

though. Time to find out. "Why isn't a guy like you married?" she asked as she filled his mug with coffee.

He seemed surprised by such a personal query. "I could ask you the same thing."

"I haven't found the right man yet," Dani said. "But I'm in the market."

He nodded. "Exactly."

Well, that sounded promising.

"The usual?" she asked with a saucy smile. "Or would you rather try something different?" She lowered her lashes a sultry fraction.

His eyes about popped out of his head before he boldly checked her out. "Define 'different.'"

"You always order the same thing for breakfast," she said. "We have lots of other delicious options. What else looks good to you?"

"You do."

By the dirty-boy gleam in his eyes, he was definitely interested.

Dani wasn't sure she cared for that and half wished she hadn't flirted with him. "Um, I mean foodwise," she said.

To her relief, Charlie calmed right down. "I like what I like, so why should I try something else? Give me the usual."

Solid and settled—that was Charlie.

She nodded. "Cheese omelet, muffin of the day and bacon, it is. I'll be right back with your orange juice."

Suddenly the door opened. A group of ranchers, all men, entered the restaurant. Sly was in the party, and so was Nick. Dani recognized everyone else, too. They were members of the local Montana Cowboy Association, and they gathered at Big Mama's twice a year for an early breakfast meeting. She'd been so preoccupied with her

Nick problems and Big Mama's stubbornness that she'd forgotten they were coming in today.

Their business was definitely appreciated—even if coming face-to-face with Nick was a little awkward.

"Hey, Dani." Sly kissed her cheek. "I heard you and Lana had fun at the house the other night."

"We did. We missed you."

Big Mama greeted everyone. She hugged both Sly and then Nick, but Dani's gaze stayed on Nick. She couldn't quite read him, but he'd barely cracked a smile at her before her mother had wrapped her arms around him.

"My boy," she said fondly. She always had loved him like a son.

Grinning, he embraced her with the same warmth as always, and Dani released a tense breath. He was acting normal now. Things must be okay.

"Dani?" Charlie called from his booth. "Can you come over here?"

"After I seat this party."

She had no idea whether he replied. She was too distracted, waiting for Nick to shine his golden grin on her. To her dismay, he gave her a cursory smile that didn't even reach his eyes.

Apparently he was as uncomfortable as she was. Their relationship was definitely off-kilter. Dani regretted those kisses more than ever. And yet, a part of her yearned for more—much more. It was all so confusing.

She greeted the other ranchers, men filled with the warmth and friendliness she'd always taken for granted with Nick.

While they seated themselves around a big table, she dropped off Charlie's food.

"I have a question for you," he said.

"Do you want a different kind of jam or more coffee?"

Charlie shook his head. "This isn't about food. It's something else."

Just now, Dani didn't want to stand around chit-chatting. "Can it wait?" she asked. "I have to take those ranchers' orders."

"Sure, I can wait."

She nodded, and moved away from the booth. Without understanding why, she snatched his carnation from the vase, stuck it behind her ear and secured it with a hair clip.

By the time she passed out menus and filled the men's mugs with coffee, they were ready to order.

Dani started with her brother. "Where'd you get that flower?" he asked.

"From Charlie over there." She nodded toward the booth where the CPA sat. "He's one of my Friday regulars. He brings me a different flower every week."

Nick's eyes grew hooded.

Not sure what to make of that, Dani addressed her brother. "What do you want to eat?"

Sly raised his eyebrows. "Are you okay, little sis?"

He knew her almost as well as she knew herself, and she couldn't get much past him.

No, she was not okay. With Nick seated at the other end of the table, she was confused and flustered. "Doing well," she said with as much enthusiasm as she could muster. "What do you want to order?"

"No small talk today, huh? I'll have the steak and eggs, with a side of hash browns and wheat toast. And keep the coffee coming. Johanna has an earache and neither Lana nor I slept much last night."

He did seem weary. "I'm sorry," Dani said.

Sly waved her words away. "Comes with the territory."

Dani moved to Frank Edison, a fiftysomething rancher

she'd met when she'd been in the high school pep squad with two of his daughters. "Ditto on the steak and eggs," Frank said. "You look real pretty with that flower behind your ear. But then, you're a pretty girl to begin with."

He'd always been nice to her, treating her almost as well as he treated his own daughters. "Thanks," Dani said.

Every man at the table echoed Frank's complimentary words. Except Nick.

"You don't care for my flower," she guessed when she was ready to take his order.

"It's fine."

Acting as if he was jealous, he crossed his arms and set his jaw. Weird.

Weirder still, Dani kind of enjoyed that. Which made her sad.

If Nick was jealous and she was happy about it, where did that leave their friendship?

The bigger question was, were they even still friends?

Dani was no longer sure. Her heart squeezed painfully. She arched her eyebrows quizically but Nick was involved in a discussion with several of the ranchers and didn't notice.

She nodded at Bill Barker, a fortysomething rancher with a wife and four young children. "How about you, Bill?" To her own ears she sounded wooden.

"I'll have the Big Mama special. Are you sure you're okay?"

She always had been an open book. Dani forced a bright smile. "I'm doing great, thanks. The special comes with your choice of a blueberry muffin or toast."

"When it comes to Big Mama's muffins, there is no choice," Bill commented.

Several men chuckled. Dani jotted down the remaining orders without any undue attention. As she left to give them to Mike, the cook, Big Mama approached her with a worried frown.

"Your face is all pinched up," she said. "What's the matter, honey?"

"Why do people keep asking me if I'm okay?" Dani snapped, earning sharp looks from Big Mama and several diners within hearing range. "I'm fine, just fine!"

Her mother glanced at the Montana Cowboy Association table, where Nick was staring at her with a crease between his brows and his lips compressed into a thin line. "What's going on between you and Nick?"

Dani longed to share the confusion and hurt with her mother, but that would mean explaining about those kisses, which she wasn't about to do. She shook her head. "I don't want to talk about it."

"Maybe you should take a break and talk to him."

Not a bad idea, except that this morning the restaurant was bustling, and Sadie and Colleen, the other waitresses, already had enough to do.

"We're too busy," she said, and hurried to turn in the ranchers' breakfast orders and refill Charlie's mug.

With Big Mama's comment about her pinched face fresh in her mind, Dani forced a pleasant expression when she topped off his coffee. "How's your breakfast today?"

"Tasty as always. You're wearing my flower behind your ear—sweet. I wanted to ask you a question, remember?"

"That's right." Dani had completely forgotten. "It's not about food, you said."

"It's about you and me. I want to take you out. What are you doing next Saturday night?"

He would ask her out when she was upset about Nick. Dani was sorry she'd encouraged him. The way she felt right now, she didn't want to go out with Charlie or any other man.

But she was eager to take action and put *something* on her weekend calendar, if only to prove to herself that she could. Besides, she reminded herself, Charlie was exactly the kind of man she wanted to date.

"I don't have anything scheduled yet," she replied.

Out of the corner of her eye, she noticed that Nick was frowning at her. She made sure her smile was nice and bright—just to make him wonder.

Assuming it was meant for him, Charlie grinned. "Now you do."

"Great," she replied with enthusiasm she didn't feel. New times, she reminded herself. "What did you have in mind?"

"For starters, dinner at Baker's." Which only happened to be the nicest, most expensive restaurant in all of Prosperity Falls. "After that…" Charlie winked. "We'll figure out something."

The wink bothered her. In no mood for sexual innuendo or any more flirtation, she glanced at the ranchers' table. "Uh-oh, my ranchers are waving for more coffee. Excuse me."

She headed for Nick's table.

"Who is that guy?" he asked, glancing at Charlie through narrowed eyes.

"That's Charlie, the man who gave me this." Dani touched the flower.

"So you said before. But who *is* he?"

She was about to explain when two women from another table gestured her over. Then several other customers wanted things, and she never did get a chance to answer Nick's question.

Charlie signaled that he was finished. When she delivered the bill he circled her wrist with his meaty thumb and forefinger. "How about giving me your phone number."

She didn't want him touching her, especially here in the restaurant. After extracting her hand, she stacked his dirty dishes. For the life of her, she couldn't bring herself to share her number with him. "I'm easiest to reach here at the restaurant," she hedged.

He nodded. "I'll call you next week and let you know when I'll be by to pick you up."

He left his usual generous tip and sauntered out.

WHAT WAS UP with Dani today? She'd had plenty of time to flirt with the bozo in the booth across the room, yet she'd barely cracked a smile Nick's way.

The strange discomfort between them bothered him. He didn't care for the tension in the air when she was near any more than he liked having the urge to reach out and touch her, as if he was staking his claim.

The way he felt right now, twitchy and tense, even a casual touch was too dangerous. As hard as he was trying to right things between them, they seemed more cockeyed than ever.

Nick needed to get home to the ranch, but not until he and Dani straightened out a few things. After the meal, he hung around, waiting for the group to break up so that he could talk with her. Before long, everyone in the Montana Cowboy Association had gone except for him and Sly. The café's entire breakfast crowd had thinned, with only a handful of diners remaining.

Dani was busy with a customer. Her brother waved goodbye, and she blew him a kiss.

As Sly made his way to the coat tree near the door, he

motioned Nick to follow him. They were the same height, and Sly looked him straight in the eyes.

"What's going on between you and my sister?" he asked in a low voice only Nick could hear.

"Nothing much."

"Uh-huh. That's why you're both so unhappy."

Nick wasn't about to discuss his problems with Dani's brother. He snorted. "Have you been smoking something you shouldn't?"

"Very funny, Kelly," Sly said, but his mouth barely quirked. "I don't care to see my sister hurt."

Seriously annoyed at the accusation, Nick squinted at Dani's brother. "How long have we known each other, Sly?"

"Awhile now."

"Sixteen years—since Dani and I first met. In all those years, have I ever hurt her?" He didn't wait for a response. "No. I would never knowingly cause her pain. Never, and for you to think otherwise..." His hands balled into fists.

"Easy, man. I'm only watching out for my little sister. Make sure that you do, too." Sly grabbed his jacket, clapped on his Stetson and left.

When Nick glanced around again, Dani was nowhere in sight. Scratching his head, he wandered over to the hostess desk.

Shelby, the weekday hostess, was close to Nick's age and about four months pregnant. Absently rubbing her lower back, she smiled at him. "Hey, Nick. How was your breakfast this morning?"

"Fantastic as always. Where's Dani?"

"She and Big Mama went into the office. I'm sure they won't mind if you go on in."

Moments later, Nick pushed through swinging doors

that led to the restrooms and the business office at the far end of the hall.

He knocked on the door and without waiting for an answer, opened it and stepped into the room.

DANI WAS SITTING across the old mahogany desk from Big Mama, the same desk that had always been there. As she caught sight of Nick, surprise colored her face.

He nodded at the older woman, then directed his gaze at Dani.

"Why, Nick, how nice of you to stick around after your meeting this morning," Big Mama said, as if he and Dani weren't staring holes in each other. "I expect you're here to talk to Dani. I should check with Mike about tomorrow's specials." She pushed heavily to her feet. "We'll go over the orders later, Dani."

Moments later the door shut behind her.

Dani didn't move from the chair. She was wearing a short skirt, tights and a sweater that emphasized her breasts. Nick kept his gaze on her big, silvery-blue eyes and sweet, kissable mouth… She was torturing him.

"Your brother just warned me not to hurt you," he said.

"He and everyone else around here should mind their own business."

"There's something we both agree on."

He expected a smile, but Dani didn't give him one. "Are you going to sit down?" she said. "Because I'm getting a crick in my neck."

There was only one empty seat in the crowded little office. Nick frowned. "You want me to sit in Big Mama's chair?"

"She won't mind."

Bills and supply orders lay across the desk. Careful

not to disturb them, he sat. "You took the carnation out from behind your ear."

Dani nodded. "Wearing it was a little weird."

"Then why did you put it on in the first place?"

"I wanted to." She bit her lip. "Charlie asked me out."

Nick had been afraid of that. He disliked the way the man had stared at Dani, as if she was dessert and he wanted to feast on her. He shook his head. "That break you're supposed to be taking from dating sure didn't last."

She blew out an irritated breath. "I said it probably wouldn't. What matters is that I'm taking a break from my usual type of man."

"Charlie's too old for you."

"He's forty. That's not so old."

"Well, he looks closer to fifty. What did you say when he asked you out?"

"That I'd go."

The thought of Charlie kissing her at the end of the evening was more than Nick could handle. "That's a bad idea," he said.

"Why? Charlie's a CPA. That's a steady job with good pay. And he hinted that he might want to settle down someday. He's exactly the kind of man I should be dating."

"But is he a decent guy?"

"He's been coming here every Friday for six months. From what I know of him, he seems to be."

Unable to argue with that, Nick gave a grudging nod. "When and where is he taking you?"

"A week from Saturday. We're going to Baker's for dinner."

"On a first date? Wow." Impressed in spite of himself, Nick whistled.

"It is pretty amazing," she said. "I have no idea what

to wear. He's complimented my brown and teal cowboy boots, but they aren't dressy enough."

"For God's sake, Dani, don't dress to please him. Dress to please yourself. If he's not happy about it, that's his problem."

Dani gave him a startled look. "Maybe I should skip your mother's wedding."

The comment from right field surprised him. "What does my mom's wedding have to do with you dating Charlie?"

"Nothing. It's just that…I get the feeling that you're in a better mood when I'm not around."

Lately, whether she was near or far away, Nick was out of sorts, but he wasn't going to admit it. "She's not getting married for another six weeks or so. Why don't you wait and decide later?"

"Okay, but if we're this uncomfortable around each other, I'm going to stay home."

The thought of them this unhappy around each other for weeks on end bummed him out. His shoulders were uncomfortably tight. In an effort to loosen up, he rolled them a couple times, which didn't do squat.

"I wish I could figure out how to get rid of this tension," he muttered.

"It's no fun, that's for sure." Dani sighed. "Our relationship is all screwed up. We never should have kissed."

Belying her own statement, she glanced at his mouth with longing written all over her face.

Nick's body jumped to life, but he was here to fix this mess, not make it worse. He tamped down his feelings— way down so that they wouldn't bubble up. "I miss my best friend."

"Me, too," Dani admitted in a soft voice.

For a long moment they stared wordlessly at each other, two confused souls at a loss what to do.

"We need to get back to where we were," she said.

He nodded. "I have to be honest here. We agreed to forget those kisses, and believe me, I've tried. But I can't stop thinking about that night."

"Tell me about it." Dani stared at her hands, locked in her lap, before again meeting his gaze. "But if we get physical, our friendship will be over for sure. And when the physical part ends, we'll be over. For good."

This was true. "We can't let that happen," Nick said.

Dani made a glum face. "We need a plan." After a moment she brightened. "Maybe if we both get involved with someone new, we'll be so interested in them that we'll stop wanting what we can't have and go back to being platonic friends."

It wasn't a bad idea—provided they each found a new partner. "I don't picture you with Charlie long-term," Nick said, and not only because imagining the guy with his hands on Dani made him see red. "There's something about him that bothers me. I can't put my finger on what it is. All I know is, I don't trust the guy."

"He may not be right for me, but I have to give him a try." She raised her head, as if resolved. "How about you, Nick? Is there someone you want to go out with?"

His thoughts flashed to Sylvie Kitchen, the redhead he'd met at Harper's Pizza. Only last night he'd tossed her business card. As soon as he got home he'd fish it out of the trash. "There is a woman I recently met. Maybe I'll take her out next weekend, while you're out with Charlie."

Dani gave a relieved nod. "Let's plan to touch bases the next day and share how it went." She glanced at the old school clock hanging above the door. "We've been talking for a while. I'm sure Big Mama is anxious to finish our meeting and go home. I know I would."

"On my way out, I'll let her know you're waiting for her." Nick stood.

Dani rose, too, and walked with him to the door. "I'm glad we talked, Nick."

"We really needed to."

Sensing that they'd get past this, that their friendship was as solid as ever, he tugged on a lock of her hair.

In return, she shot him a dazzling smile that transformed her whole face. She was so beautiful, his chest ached. He reached for the door with a shaky hand.

"Wait," Dani said.

Standing on her toes, she planted a chaste kiss on his cheek, the same as she always had.

But this felt different. Sweeter.

The scent of her orange blossom shampoo made him want to bury his face in her hair. Then tilt up her chin and ramp up the kiss into something a whole lot hotter.

Nick stifled a groan. It was all he could do not to act on his fierce need. But his future friendship with Dani depended on behaving himself.

Unaware of the torture she was putting him through, she almost smiled. "We're going to be okay," she said. "I know it."

Not at all convinced, Nick nodded and walked through the door.

Chapter Six

"Do Sadie and Colleen need a hand?" Dani asked when Big Mama returned to the office. Sadie had waitressed at the restaurant for over twenty years, and Colleen for five.

Dani's mother shook her head. "Right now, we're not too busy." She moved toward her desk more slowly than Dani could ever remember. "You're much happier than you were when I left. I'm guessing that whatever was bothering you and Nick has been settled," she said, her smile at odds with her lumbering movements.

She sat down cautiously, as if she were sore or in pain. Earlier, she'd gotten up the same way.

"Do your legs hurt?" Dani asked, concerned.

"At my age, everything hurts."

Big Mama chuckled, but Dani found nothing funny about the little joke. For the past few days, her vibrant mother had become noticeably less energetic. Age, Dani assumed. She hated that Big Mama was getting older. "You're in pain," she said, "and I don't like it."

"Just you wait until you're sixty-nine, missy. You'll have your share of aches and pains, too. I assume I mentioned your upcoming date with Charlie to Nick. Does he approve?"

"I'm not talking about that until you tell me what's wrong."

"At times you can be so stubborn and exasperating," her mother muttered. "There's nothing wrong. My knees bother me, but that's been going on for years now. Yes, I'm tired today, but only because I didn't sleep well last night." She widened her eyes. "Does that satisfy you, missy, or would you prefer that I go into minute detail and bore us both to death?"

"Now who's exasperating?" Dani said. They both smiled. "I can guess why you couldn't sleep. You're worried about the restaurant."

Her mother's eyes flashed. *Bingo.*

"Things have been pretty slow," she conceded. "But tourist season is just around the corner, and things are bound to pick up."

"We can hope, but we have so much competition now, and not just from the Poplar Tree. If we address our problems now, we'll have a better chance of boosting our business no matter what the season. The restaurant could use a facelift and a few new—"

Her mother cut her off with a glare. "Big Mama's Café is fine the way it is," she insisted. "If you must know, the real reason why I couldn't sleep last night is because I had a bad case of indigestion."

Not finished the restaurant discussion, Dani crossed her arms. "You can't keep pretending that our problems here will just go away. They won't, and we have to be realistic. Sooner or later, we have to make some changes. Otherwise…"

Hoping to worry her mother into taking action, she let the ominous implications hang between them. The only indication that Big Mama heard was the slight tightening of her jaw.

Several tense seconds ticked by before Dani mentally

threw up her hands and changed the subject. "Nick's mom is getting married again," she said. "She wants me to go."

"She's having *another* wedding?"

"Nothing fancy this time. They're using a justice of the peace."

Her mother nodded. "You and Nick are such close friends, it makes sense that she'd want you there."

Up until now they'd been very close, anyway. But if they didn't move past their attraction to each other, any future relationship was doomed.

Unfortunately Dani was completely fixated on Nick, and not just as a friend. That had to change. She wasn't sure why she'd kissed him on the cheek earlier. Maybe to test herself. A dangerous test she'd nearly failed. For a few minutes there, it had taken all her strength not to slant his head toward her and kiss his mouth instead.

But kissing Nick the way she longed to was out. Now and forever.

"What did you eat for dinner last night?" she asked in a desperate push to tamp down her desire for him.

"Fried chicken, biscuits and gravy."

Dani's mouth watered. Her mother made killer fried chicken and side dishes. "Eating all that rich food—no wonder you had indigestion. Dr. Adelson warned you to cut down on foods that are high in fat and cholesterol. We all should. That's one reason why I believe we should offer healthier menu options for our customers." Big Mama's lips thinned in warning—the stubborn woman wasn't going to discuss even that—and Dani returned to last night's dinner. "I don't suppose you had any vegetables or a salad with your meal?"

Her mother made a face. "No, I didn't. Now you can answer my question. What's Nick's opinion of you and Charlie?"

Dani eyed her mother. "We haven't finished talking about you and your diet."

"Yes, we have." Big Mama's mulish expression signaled that that subject was indeed closed.

A second topic shut down. Seriously annoyed, Dani lashed out. "You won't discuss the restaurant and you won't talk about your diet. And you call me stubborn. You're so hard-headed, I could scream!"

"Please don't. It might upset our lunch customers. What did Nick say about your date with Charlie?"

Dani gave up arguing with her mother—for now. "He doesn't care for Charlie. He thinks he's too old for me."

With the flick of her hand, Big Mama disposed of that opinion. "That just means he's had more time to mature and settle into his CPA career. And a fine career it is. He's a good prospect, Dani. I'm pleased that you're following through on your plan to date someone different from your usual choices."

Although Dani smiled, she couldn't summon up much enthusiasm for her upcoming date. She wanted so much to be excited, wanted to like Charlie so that she'd stop wanting Nick.

"You're frowning," Big Mama said.

"Just making a mental list of the supplies I should order for next week."

Her mother nodded. "After talking with Mike, I know just what we need. Let's make that list. Then we can both get back to work."

As CHARLIE HAD PROMISED, on Tuesday he called Dani at the restaurant. "I remembered that you have to get up early on Sunday, so I made our dinner reservation for six-thirty," he said. "Since it's outside the city limits and will take about thirty minutes to get there, I'll pick you up at six."

"All right," Dani said, hoping she sounded more excited than she was. Pushing away her dread—this date *had* to work—she gave him her address.

When she hung up, Sadie leaned in close. "You look as thrilled as a woman about to have bunion surgery. Are you sure you want to go out with Charlie?"

Dani loved the down-to-earth woman. "Is my lack of enthusiasm that obvious? And here I figured I was so convincing."

"Not with that long face. You mentioned you're trying to date a different kind of man, but I don't understand why you picked Charlie. He doesn't seem like your type."

"That's the whole point," Dani said. "He's the complete opposite of the guys I usually go for."

"Yes, but…" Sadie shook her head. "Never mind. What do I know? I've been married and divorced three times, twice with the same man."

"That just about makes you an expert," Dani teased. "What were you going to say?"

"Charlie has never been anything but polite in here, but there's something about him that bothers me. For the life of me, I can't put my finger on what it is, though."

Nick had said something similar.

Nick. The whole reason Dani had said yes to Charlie. No, this date wasn't just about Nick. It was for her, too. She wanted a man with a real job, who respected her and treated her well. If this date worked out and they continued to see each other, who knew where it would lead? Her feelings for Charlie could change for the better.

"Maybe it's because he tries so hard to make everyone like him," Sadie went on. "If he'd just relax, he might be more appealing."

"Could be," Dani said, striving to convince herself. "He's taking me to Baker's."

"Really! I've never been lucky enough to go there."

"I've been twice. Once with my date for senior prom—" she and Nick had double-dated "—and once for my twenty-first birthday." Big Mama and Nick had treated her.

She glanced across the restaurant at her mother, who was rubbing her chest and leaning heavily on the order counter.

For almost a week now, Dani had been concerned for her. Now she was plain-out worried. She lowered her voice so that only Sadie could hear. "Does Big Mama seem okay to you?"

Sadie wrinkled her nose. "Not really. Today she seems especially blah, and I don't like it. She's pale, too, similar to my daughter when she has the flu. I wonder if she's coming down with something."

"She never gets sick," Dani said. "But if she did, she'd stay home."

While Sadie locked the restaurant door some minutes later, Dani confronted her mother. "You keep rubbing your chest," she pointed out.

"It's just a little heartburn."

"You've got to start eating right. You should see Dr. Adelson."

"What for? He'll just tell me what I already know. I don't need another of his lectures on what I should and shouldn't eat."

Dani swallowed a sigh. "Will you at least schedule a physical?"

"I'm fine."

"No, you aren't. You're pale and tired, and you keep rubbing your chest."

"For heaven's sake, quit worrying about me! I'm strong as an ox."

"Please get a physical. If not for yourself, do it for me."

"And just where would I find the time?"

"That's why you have me," Dani said. "I run the restaurant on weekends. I can certainly run it for a few more hours while you're at the doctor's."

"I already take off Saturdays and Sundays. I can't afford to take any more days off."

If she trusted Dani, she wouldn't be so reluctant.

In Dani's life, she'd had precious little of that. First she'd lost her parents and the implicit trust that they would always be there. Then she'd lost her brothers for umpteen years. Add in all the guys who'd broken her heart, and trust was in short supply.

Certainly she trusted Big Mama—why couldn't her mother do the same? She'd done everything possible to prove she could handle the restaurant. She kept things running smoothly and efficiently and handled any emergencies as well as her mother. But this was not the moment to bring that up.

"Then schedule a Monday appointment. But please, for my own peace of mind, get yourself checked."

Her mother tightened her lips.

"If you don't call Dr. Adelson, I will," Dani threatened.

That did the trick. Big Mama expelled an irritated breath and gave in. "All right, Dani, all right! I'll make an appointment."

WITH EARLY SPRING in full force, there was plenty to do on the ranch. For several days, Nick alternated between the never-ending task of mending the fences that had fallen into disrepair over the winter and helping inseminate heifers and cows. The spring grass was starting to come up. In another week or two it would be lush and ripe. Grazing on the nutrient-rich grass enabled his cattle to put on weight—faster and more economically than feeding them hay and artificial vitamins and minerals. The more weight they gained, the better. Fat, healthy animals fetched top dollar at the spring market.

After chores late Saturday afternoon, he showered and dressed for his date with Sylvie Kitchen. They had a dinner reservation at Baker's, the same restaurant where Charlie was taking Dani.

Dani wouldn't be pleased about that, but Nick wanted to keep an eye on the CPA.

Just after six he pulled up to Sylvie's house. She lived in a well-maintained cottage in a nice area.

She answered the door wearing a soft pink dress that clung to her curves and heels that made her legs impossibly long, putting her almost at eye-level with him.

"You look fantastic," he said.

"Thank you."

She favored him with a warm smile that should have rocked his world. It didn't.

On the drive to the restaurant they chatted easily.

"How long have you been a rancher, Nick?" she asked.

"I was born on Kelly Ranch, but when I was nine my family sold it. Then a couple years ago, I bought it back."

Sylvie nodded. "I had a distant cousin who owned a ranch, but he ended up selling it. Ranching isn't easy."

"It can be a real challenge, but it's in my blood," Nick said. "What about you, Sylvie? What's your story?"

She told him about her very normal life, which included the kind of carefree childhood Nick had always dreamed about. Her parents were still happily married, and she was close to her brother and sister, who were both married with kids.

She was poised, smart, beautiful and a decent conversationalist. Nick liked her.

But she wasn't Dani.

Wasn't that the whole point?

Chapter Seven

Charlie arrived at exactly 6:00 p.m. Dani buzzed him up. When he knocked on the door a few minutes later, she pasted a smile on her face and let him in. "Hi, Charlie."

In a suit and tie, he was almost handsome. The scent of Old Spice clung heavily to him.

"I like that suit," she said.

"Thanks." His gaze darted over her. "Nice dress."

Remembering the sexual glint in his eyes that day at the restaurant, she'd chosen flats and a loose blue sheath that played down her curves. To further hide her body, she'd looped the colorful silk scarf she'd painted in art class around her shoulders. Yet by Charlie's overly warm expression she might just as well have worn a snug mini-dress and do-me heels.

Dani didn't like that, and wondered what his expectations were for later tonight. Over dinner she'd set him straight.

"Did you have any trouble finding the building?" she asked.

"None."

There the conversation ended. As the silence stretched out, Charlie stuck his hand in his pocket and jiggled his change. No signs of sexual interest now. Clearly he was nervous.

When Fluff came running to meet him, Dani heaved a sigh of relief and sent a big thanks to her cat for making an appearance at exactly the right moment. "This is my cat, Fluff," she said.

Instead of greeting or petting the tom, her date stepped back.

"You're not a cat person?" Dani asked.

"I'm allergic. They make me sneeze."

So much for Fluff. "We should go."

She opened the closet and took out her dress coat, the one she wore to weddings and other special occasions. His gentleman gene showing, Charlie helped her into it.

As the elevator descended to the lobby, Dani vowed to do everything she could to put Charlie at ease. Otherwise she was in for a long, uncomfortable evening.

His new-model sedan was neat and clean, and the radio was tuned to her favorite country station. This was good.

Steve Belong was singing "Little Red Dress." "I love the beat of this song," she said, singing along for a few bars.

Charlie gave her a look she couldn't decipher. "You don't want me to sing?" she asked.

"Not really. I can't hear the music."

Dani stopped. She asked him who his favorite singers were. To her relief, he opened up a little. They discussed music and discovered they shared a taste for blues as well as country. Charlie mentioned an upcoming concert, and Dani assumed that if the date went well, he would probably invite her to go with him.

Some thirty minutes later, a smiling hostess led them to their table. Baker's was a whole different world from Big Mama's Café, but Dani absorbed every detail to mull over later. Music floated through the air, pleasant but not intrusive. Diners filled almost every table. Soft lighting, fresh flowers in crystal vases and off-white linens gave the restaurant a romantic air.

"What do you like to do for fun?" Dani asked as she and Charlie sipped cocktails.

"I'm big into fishing." Having grown more comfortable with her—or maybe it was the alcohol—Charlie launched into stories about fishing with his buddies, fellow Elks Club members in Missoula, where he'd lived before relocating to Prosperity.

Charlie ordered another drink. Dani declined.

"Why did you move here?" she asked while he drank it.

"I got a great job offer. Also, because of the Ames and Missouri Rivers in town. After the tax season, my buddies are planning to drive over. We'll fish in both."

He talked at length about his hobby—the various lures he used, how he determined which to use, and when. Then, in copious detail, he launched into how he'd built a smoker for the trout and salmon he caught. He explained how to season the fish and how to test when they were fully smoked. And on and on, without barely a pause, until Dani's eyes nearly crossed. She half wished he were still too nervous to talk.

The first course, a squash soup, was smooth and delicious despite the company. Although Charlie hardly seemed to notice the food. Instead of commenting on the dish, he kept on talking, never pausing long enough for Dani to comment, and never asking her a single question about herself. As if a pipe had burst, with no shutoff valve.

She stopped listening and glanced frequently and obviously at her watch in hopes that he would take the hint and either shut his mouth or ask for the check—neither of which he did—when to her surprise, Nick moved into her line of sight.

On his arm, a stunning redhead. As far as she knew, he rarely brought a date here. For a moment she wondered if he'd picked this restaurant because she'd said she would be here with Charlie.

Regardless, he certainly hadn't wasted any time finding someone new. She was gorgeous, too, sleek and slender. Dani didn't have a sleek bone in her body.

A funny feeling churned in her gut. Jealousy.

As if sensing her gaze, Nick looked straight at her. He steered his date toward their table. Dani managed a smile.

"Hey, Dani," he said. "Funny running into you here. Nice scarf."

Not so funny, when he'd known she would be here, but she refrained from pointing that out. "It's the one I made at the silk painting class." She pivoted toward the redhead. "I'm Dani Pettit."

"Sylvie Kitchen." Sylvie held out her hand.

"Dani's an old friend of mine," Nick said.

"He means longtime. We're not old," Dani joked.

Polite laughter all around.

"Nick and Sylvie, meet Charlie."

Charlie nodded at Nick. "I saw you at Big Mama's last week. You came in with a bunch of guys."

Nick nodded. "We had a ranchers' meeting. We do that at Big Mama's twice a year."

"I'm a CPA. We sometimes have breakfast meetings, too." Charlie ogled Sylvie and gave her a wolfish smile.

All guys looked at women, but blatantly checking someone out and flirting with her in front of Dani and the other woman's date? Charlie's crude behavior reminded her all too well of a couple of her previous boyfriends.

And cemented the doubts that had been forming since he'd picked her up. Heck, since he'd first asked her out.

He definitely wasn't for her.

The hostess came over. "Mr. Kelly and Miss Kitchen, your table is ready. Unless you'd prefer to join this table?"

Nick shook his head. "No, thanks. Good to meet you, Charlie." Moments later, he and Sylvie sat down on the opposite side of the restaurant.

"That's some redhead your friend is with," Charlie said with an admiring shake of his head. "She could be Miss America."

A little envious of the woman, Dani nodded. "Everyone Nick dates is pretty." Although Sylvie was downright stunning. No doubt he was eager to make her his new girlfriend.

The main course arrived. Neither she nor Charlie spoke for a while.

This course was also delicious, but Dani picked at her meal. Her pang of jealousy turned into full-fledged heartache. Silently she chastised herself. Wasn't this what she and Nick both wanted—to meet someone who made them forget each other? She was happy for him. She was.

Charlie looked concerned, and Dani realized she was frowning. "Hey, you're pretty, too," he said, smiling at her.

Too little, too late.

If Charlie realized she was irritated with him, he didn't let on. "You two used to be involved, huh?"

"No," Dani told him. "As we explained, we're friends."

He gave a sly smile. "The kind with benefits."

"Nope. We've always been close, but ours is a platonic friendship." At least she intended for it to be once again, just as soon as she found a man who interested her.

Nick seemed to be on the right track. With any luck, Dani would catch up soon.

Right now, though, she just wanted to go home. But Charlie was only halfway through his meal.

"So what's Nick doing at Baker's tonight?" he asked.

Dani glanced at his table, where a waiter was delivering soups. "From what I can see, he's about to have dinner with his date."

"Yeah, then why does he keep staring over here?"

Dani glanced at Nick's table and caught him doing just that. She gave him a dirty look and returned her attention to Charlie.

Within ten minutes, his plate was empty. "You ready for coffee and dessert?" he asked.

Although Dani was too full for another bite, she figured Charlie wasn't. "Sure."

Soon after Charlie finished his chocolate meringue pie—and hers—he signaled for the check.

"Let's get out of here," he said, with a heavy-lidded expression that was definitely sexual.

Was he kidding? Intending to put out that fire right now, she eyed him with cool disinterest. "Listen, I have to be up at four-thirty tomorrow. I need to get home."

"Yeah, okay."

The gleam faded from his eyes. Dismissing her misgivings, she pushed her chair away from the table.

It was a relief to know that he understood.

BY THE TIME Nick pulled up at Sylvie's, it was starting to rain. He took her arm and moved quickly to her door. "Don't want to get those pretty shoes wet," he said, his breath clouding in front of him.

"Right," she said.

"We made it," he said as they ducked under the eaves

and the soft porch light. When she didn't reply, he frowned. "You've been awfully quiet since we left Baker's."

"Have I? Baker's has always been one of my favorite restaurants. I enjoyed our dinner, Nick."

"Me, too." He wasn't lying. Sylvie was easy to talk to.

The welcoming warmth in her gaze assured him that she wouldn't fight a good-night kiss. Happy to oblige, he leaned in and brushed his lips over hers.

It was a decent kiss, but nothing special. He stepped back.

"It's Dani, isn't it?" Sylvie said. "You're hung up on her."

Nick added "smart" to the list of things he liked about this woman. She was right—he definitely was hung up on Dani.

But damn it, that was going to change.

"As Dani and I said earlier, we've known each other a long time—since high school," he said. "We're friends, but that's all."

"That's not what I saw. The way you looked at her, and the warmth in her eyes when she looked at you… The old 'sparks flew' cliché comes to mind. Then, all during dinner, you kept watching her. You tried to be covert about it, but I noticed."

Busted. Damn.

Nick shifted his weight. "That was rude. I owe you an apology and an explanation. The truth is, until a few weeks ago, Dani and I *were* platonic friends. It's been that way for sixteen years. We were happy with our relationship.

"Then without either of us meaning for it to happen, things changed." Not about to get into that, he cut to the chase. "We want to be in that friends-only place again, so we're dating other people."

"We," she murmured.

"What did you say?"

"You keep saying 'we,' as if you and Dani are a couple."

In a sense, they were, but not the way Sylvie thought. "I mean 'we' as friends," Nick said.

His date brushed the words aside with a *what kind of fool do you take me for?* look. "Let's see if I understand correctly. To help you and Dani regain your friendship-only status, you asked me out, and Dani went out with Charlie."

Nick nodded. "That's it in a nutshell. But that's not the whole reason I asked you out. You're an attractive woman and I wanted to get to know you better. I'm glad I did. I like you, Sylvie."

Pensive, she frowned, her forehead slightly furrowed. "Don't you think your plan would have worked better if you'd chosen different restaurants instead of showing up at the same one, at the same time?"

Nick scrubbed the back of his neck. "That was totally my fault. Dani told me where she and Charlie were going. She had no idea that I'd show up."

"Why did you take me there, Nick?" Sylvie asked.

"It's a great place to bring a date."

"Yes, but why, really?"

"Because I don't trust Charlie."

"In other words, you wanted to keep an eye on Dani." Sylvie gave him a smile that was devoid of any humor. "You don't think she can take care of herself?"

If Dani heard that, she'd bean him. "I'm sure she can," he said. "But in case there was trouble, I wanted to be there. I didn't just take you to Baker's so that I could keep an eye on her," he added. "I meant what I said, Sylvie—

I enjoyed having dinner with you. You're intelligent and beautiful—a terrific date."

She was silent a moment. "And yet, your plan to distract yourself with my company didn't work."

Put that way, he sounded like a real jerk. He pointed to his face. "If you want to slap me, go ahead. I deserve it."

"I'm considering it." Her lips twitched. "At least I got a first-rate meal out of this."

Her ability to tease him after what he'd done made him sorry that he didn't feel more for her. He touched her cheek. "You're an amazing woman, you know that?"

"As a matter of fact, I do." She gave him a genuine smile. "Explain something to me, Nick. Why don't you and Dani just give in and let your relationship go where it wants to?"

"Because mixing sex and friendship won't work for either of us. Once we cross over to the physical side of things, our friendship will become a thing of the past. We don't want to lose what we have now."

"Now I'm really confused," Sylvie said. "Can't you have sex and continue to be friends?"

"That wouldn't work for us. Dani usually falls for every guy she sleeps with. Her relationships never last, and she gets hurt a lot. I'm not great at relationships, either, and I don't fall in love. I don't want to hurt her."

Sylvie studied him. "Your saying that even if Dani wasn't in the picture, you and I wouldn't have a future."

Not about to lie, he nodded. "As much as I like you, I'm not looking for a committed relationship. I was going to explain that tonight, only I didn't get around to it."

"That's too bad. I'd hoped that maybe…" Sylvie's words trailed off. "Oh, well."

"Hey, you can do a whole lot better than me. You're special, and you deserve a guy who'll give you the moon."

"That's sweet, and very romantic. I hope you and Dani work things out."

Nick hoped so, too. He kissed Sylvie's cheek and wished her a great life. As soon as she headed inside, he left.

He intended to drive straight to the ranch, climb into bed and sleep. A gut feeling he couldn't ignore or explain stopped him.

Dani was in trouble. He sped toward her place.

Chapter Eight

On the drive home after dinner, it started raining. Charlie was quiet, and the only sounds in the car were the wipers and the radio.

Dani didn't mind. After his nonstop monologue all evening, the silence was a welcome change. She didn't say a word until he pulled into the parking lot. "You don't have to park, Charlie, just let me out here, by the front door. Thanks for tonight. I'll see you at Big Mama's on Friday."

Acting as if he hadn't heard her, he angled into a slot in the Visitor Parking area.

"I'd rather you didn't walk me to the door," she said to make sure he understand that she wasn't up for a kiss.

Charlie set the brake on his car. Had he not heard her? "I have to get up at four-thirty, remember?" she said. "You're not walking me to my door and you can't come up. If you drive around to the entrance, I can dash inside without getting wet."

Her words fell on deaf ears. He killed the engine.

So much for staying dry. "Well, good night," Dani said, reaching for the door handle.

He put his hand over hers, stopping her. "Don't go yet, Dani. You haven't given me my kiss."

His voice was low and warm. Sexual. Apparently, he

hadn't gotten the message that she wasn't into him. "Listen, Charlie, I think you're a nice guy, but I'm not interested in you that way," she said in an effort to let him down gently.

"Then let me be your friend with benefits, like Nick."

He would mention Nick. "As I've explained twice before, it isn't that way between him and me. I don't want to kiss you or do anything else," she stated, not so gently now.

"One kiss and you'll change your mind."

"I'm certain I won't."

"I want my kiss."

It was clear that he wouldn't let her leave until she complied. "All right, Charlie, one small kiss. No tongue."

She leaned across the gap between the seats for a quick peck, but he cupped the back of her head so that she couldn't move away. Then he forced his tongue in her mouth.

"Don't," she said, struggling to get away.

His grip on her only tightened. "Come on, Dani, give it a chance."

"What part of 'I'm not interested in you' don't you understand? Let. Go. Of. Me."

"Not yet." Now his hands were under her coat, clasping her waist. "Taking you to Baker's cost me a bundle, and you don't even invite me up? I want something in exchange for tonight and for those flowers and big tips I've been leaving you for months."

Shock rendered her speechless. In the distance, thunder growled ominously.

Charlie tried to kiss her again. She slapped him so hard, her palm stung.

Instead of reeling back, he laughed. "I like a girl with spunk."

Who'd have guessed that the mild-mannered CPA was a certifiable nutcase? "I took a self-defense class last year," she warned.

It hadn't actually been a class, just an hour-long, free introductory lesson given as a preview of the full six-week session. At the time, Dani had decided not to sign up. Now she wished she had.

"Did you?" Charlie let go of her waist and squeezed both her hands in his. "Just try fooling around with me, Dani. You might be surprised at how much you enjoy it. I have a big you-know-what, and he's ready for action. He wants you to play with him."

He pushed her hands toward his erection.

More scared that she could ever remember, Dani elbowed him in the chest. Hard.

"Oof," he said, and released her.

She grabbed for the door, but Charlie was faster. "Don't fight me, Dani. You know you want it."

"I'd rather eat a cow pie."

"You little tease." Charlie reclined his seat all the way down and attempted to pull her onto his lap.

She resisted, started to scream, but he muffled her voice with a wet kiss. Gagging and tasting bile, Dani did the only thing she could think of. She bit his tongue.

"Ow!" He let go of her.

She was scrambling off his lap when the driver's seat door jerked open.

"Get your hands off her," a threatening voice ordered.

Nick's voice. He was here.

Relief washed over her as she shot out of the passenger side of the car. Safe now and breathing hard, she sagged against a cold steel post. Rain she barely noticed pelted her head.

Nick's gaze flitted over her open coat and rumpled

dress, and something hardened in his face. "Are you hurt?" he asked, his gentle tone at odds with his fisted hands.

Other than being terrified, she was unharmed. "I'm okay."

"That's good. It means I don't have to beat the crap out of this bastard."

Nick hauled Charlie out of the car by the lapels of his suit jacket and set him down some feet away. Then he got in Charlie's face. He spoke too softly for Dani to hear his words.

Hands up and palms out, Charlie scuttled backward toward his sedan. When he bumped into the hood, Nick pushed him toward the open driver's door.

"Get out of here," he growled.

Without a word Charlie jumped into the car and slammed the door shut. The locks clicked. Seconds later, he peeled off.

As Nick moved toward Dani, a fresh clap of thunder rattled the air. "You sure you're all right?" he said.

She nodded. "How did you know to show up here?"

"Something told me that you needed me. You're shivering."

She was, Dani realized.

He shrugged out of his overcoat and placed it over hers, around her shoulders. It was warm and smelled just like Nick.

Lightning crackled in the sky, and another shower of angry rain battered the ground.

"Come on." He grasped her hand and pulled her toward the entrance of the apartment building. With a hand that trembled, Dani entered the code.

Wet and slightly winded, they entered the empty lobby. It was always too hot, but tonight Dani welcomed the warmth. She couldn't seem to stop shivering. Or let go of Nick's hand.

Using his free hand, he tucked her hair behind her ears with infinite tenderness that calmed her raw nerves.

"You're freezing," he said in a gruff voice. "Come here."

Dani stepped into his warmth and held on tight. His arms around her were exactly what she needed. Closing her eyes, she sighed.

"That's my girl." Nick kissed the top of her head and then released her. "Maybe we should call the sheriff's office."

"What would I say? That Charlie tried something? He wasn't the first."

Although he'd been the first who'd tried to force her.

"Just to get what he did on record, in case he tries the same thing on someone else. You ought to tell someone so that it doesn't happen again. I'll confirm your story."

As badly as Dani wanted to forget what had happened, she knew Nick was right. "Okay," she said. "I'll do it right now."

"Why don't you wait until you're in your apartment?"

She shook her head. "I want to get it over with."

She handed him his coat, then sat down on the lobby couch, pulled out her phone and made the call. After a brief conversation, she hung up. "According to the sheriff's office, since nothing really serious happened—" Dani shuddered at the very suggestion of Charlie doing something scarier "—I can't file a report. The officer I spoke with gave me the name and number of a place to contact if I need to talk to someone."

"It was worth a shot," Nick said. "Come on, I'll take you upstairs."

Now that she was calmer, questions flooded her mind.

"How did you figure out where to find me?" she asked while they waited for the elevator.

"Easy. You have to be up early tomorrow, and I guessed you'd come home straight from dinner."

That made sense. "First you show up at the same restaurant as me. Now you're here. Are you stalking me?"

His mouth quirked. "That's me, all right. I was at Baker's for the same reason I'm here now—because I had a gut instinct about Charlie. And a lucky thing I did."

The elevator arrived. He reached for her hand and pulled her into the car. Dani held on tightly.

"Charlie won't bother you anymore," he said on the ride to the seventh floor.

She let go of his hand and hugged her waist. "How can you be sure?"

"For one thing, I had a hard time understanding a word he said because you bit the hell out of his tongue. Smart move, by the way. Did you learn that at that self-defense demo you went to last year?"

"I have no idea where it came from," she said. "I just did it."

"You should get in touch with the woman who does those demos and explain so that she can teach others."

"I will. I think I'll sign up for that class, too."

"Smart idea."

"What did you say to Charlie in the parking lot?" she asked.

"Nothing much. Let's just say, he understands that if he so much as speaks to you again, I'll come after him. Also I might have mentioned that Sheriff Dean is a friend of mine."

"He is not."

"So I stretched the truth a little. We did talk once when he stopped me for speeding." His mouth twitched.

The elevator stopped. Nick accompanied her down the hall. He stood at her side while she found her key and unlocked the door.

Dani meant to say good-night, but completely different words came out of her mouth. "I wouldn't mind company for a while."

"I was coming in regardless."

INSIDE DANI'S APARTMENT, Nick tossed his own coat aside and helped her out of hers. Her fingers were ice cold, likely more from the fear Charlie had caused than the chilly night air.

Rage filled him. He wanted to go out, find the bastard and pound him into the ground so that he'd pay for what he'd tried with Dani and would never try to force any woman to do things she didn't want to do. But beating Charlie to a pulp wouldn't solve anything. Besides, Dani didn't want to be alone.

She prided herself on her strength and independence and shied away from showing any weakness. But she needed him, and he intended to stay for as long as she wanted him here.

With a meow, Fluff came running. Tears filled Dani's eyes, tears Nick knew she didn't want him to see.

"Hey, Fluff." She picked up the cat and buried her face in his fur.

Nick wanted to pull her close again and rub her shoulders or massage her feet. Anything to help her relax and feel better. But she wouldn't appreciate it if he babied her.

"You're wet from the rain," he said. "You should take a warm shower, and I could use something hot to drink. You wouldn't by chance have any of that homemade cocoa mix?"

That cheered her up. "Cocoa sounds perfect. It just so happens that I made up a batch the other day."

"I'll fix the cocoa while you shower."

Ten minutes later, Dani entered the kitchen wearing flannel pajamas, a pink fleece robe and fuzzy pink slippers. She'd blown her hair dry, and her face had some color to it. Fluff was with her.

"All better?" Nick asked.

"I'm definitely warmer."

"That's good. The cocoa is just about ready."

While Nick finished up, Fluff settled on the mini rug Dani kept for him near the heat register.

They took their steaming mugs to the living room and sat on the couch, Dani close beside him. Exactly as they'd been the night they'd fallen asleep together and their troubles had started. Nick wouldn't think about that now. Tonight he only wanted her to feel safe.

"Mmm, this is yummy," she said, sounding more like herself. But tension still radiated from her, holding her body rigid. "I hope your date ended better than mine."

Nick shrugged. "It was okay."

"Not so great, huh? Sylvie seemed nice, Nick. She's beautiful, too."

"And smart. But she's not the woman for me."

"Not even for a little while?"

He shook his head. "She wants the kind of relationship I can't give. She knows it, too."

Dani plucked a turquoise throw pillow from beside her and hugged it. "I guess it's back to the drawing board for both of us. Tell me something. What was it about Charlie that bothered you?"

"He leered at you like a dirty old man. It bugged me. And the flower thing—he had no business doing that every week."

She eyed him. "There's nothing wrong with a man bringing me a flower. You almost sound jealous."

"Hey, if he'd been a decent guy, I would have been okay with it."

That wasn't wholly true. Sure, he wanted Dani to find someone who could make her happy. But at the same time, he couldn't stand the idea of sharing her with any man. Whatever the hell that meant. He'd never felt this way before and knew his jealousy—or whatever the hell it was—had something to do with those kisses. But he wasn't about to analyze himself.

"I'm beginning to wonder if there are any decent guys out there," Dani said. "I went out with a freaking CPA, and it turned into the worst date ever. Also the scariest."

A shudder passed through her. Nick set his mug on the coffee table and put his arm around her. "It's all behind you now."

She stared up at him and bit her lip. "What if he comes into Big Mama's?"

Nick's protective hackles rose all over again, along with his rage. "You tell Big Mama, Sadie, Colleen, Mike and everyone else at the restaurant what happened tonight. They'll make sure Charlie doesn't come in. But if he does, call the sheriff immediately. Then call me."

"I will. Thanks for making me feel safe, Nick."

He tightened his arm around her, and she snuggled against him. No sign of that stiffness now. Nick smiled to himself. "You finally relaxed."

"Because of you. This is going to sound weird, but if tonight hadn't turned out the way it did, I wouldn't have my best friend back." Her silvery-blue eyes were wide and trusting, just as they used to be.

Relieved, and feeling as if he'd come home again, Nick silently pledged that he would never let Dani down.

"Remember when you came to Big Mama's for your Montana Cowboy meeting a couple weeks ago?" she asked.

"How could I forget? That was the first time I laid eyes on Charlie."

Dani tensed again, and Nick wished he'd kept his mouth shut.

"Did you notice anything about Big Mama?" she asked.

"She seemed to be moving more slowly than usual, I guess. Why?"

"I'm worried about her, Nick. She isn't sleeping well. She claims indigestion is keeping her awake, but what if it's her heart?"

Alarmed, he sat up straight. "Has she seen her doctor?"

"She promised to make an appointment, but I doubt she has."

"Stubborn lady. I'll give her a call and nudge her."

"Would you? Thanks."

In comfortable silence they finished their cocoas.

Dani sighed up at him. "Our plan to meet new love interests isn't going so well, is it?"

"Not so far," he agreed. "But you and I are tight again. I missed that. Missed you."

"Me, too." She let out a contented sound and burrowed closer.

Warm and soft, with her hair smelling of orange blossoms. A few silky strands teased his chin. He brushed them away, his fingers lingering on her smooth skin.

His body stirred, ready for action it wasn't going to get. Not with Dani.

Calling himself every bad name in the book, Nick warned himself to move away, before he blew everything and kissed her. But she seemed so comfortable and content that he stayed put. Leaning his head against the wall behind the couch, he stared at the dark TV screen instead of Dani.

"What are you thinking about?" she asked.

He glanced down at her, just in time to see her tongue lick some cocoa from the corner of her lip.

Did she have any idea what she was doing to him?

Damn it, she'd been through hell tonight. What kind of jerk was he to want her now?

A big one. He was so intent on her lush mouth that he had to struggle to pull his thoughts together. If he told her what was on his mind, the things he wanted to do with her, their newly resurrected platonic friendship would be toast.

Hell, for him it already was.

Forget how comfortable and relaxed Dani was. Nick had to move. Now.

"It's getting late, and you have to be up early. I should go." He pulled his arm from around her and stood. "Unless you want me to stay over."

Had he just offered to stay here all night? He must be losing his mind. "I can sleep on the couch."

Dani's gaze connected with his, and he swore he saw yearning on her face. Real, or wishful thinking? Because if she encouraged him in any way, he wasn't sure he could resist.

To his relief, she shook her head. "I'm better now."

Nick let out the breath he'd been holding. "Okay, but if you change your mind, if you need anything at all, call me."

"I will." At the door, she managed a smile. "Thanks again, Nick, for being here when I really needed you."

"Sure. Sweet dreams."

"I love that you said that—just as you always have. Right back at ya, my best friend." Standing on her toes, she cupped his face in her soft hands and kissed his cheek. The same as she had the other day, after their talk in Big Mama's office.

He'd had trouble resisting her then, and it was worse now.

The warmth in her eyes and the sweetness of that chaste kiss burned and rippled through him, and it was all he could do to suffer through it without hauling her up nice and close and giving in to his desires.

"I'll check on you tomorrow," he said in a voice that sounded ragged to his own ears. Then he made a quick exit.

Chapter Nine

After spending a restless night tossing and turning, Nick woke to clear skies Sunday morning. At some point during the night the rain had stopped. This morning the winter chill was absent. The weather had definitely changed—a welcome change for him and all the ranchers in Prosperity. It was almost time to move his cattle into the grazing pastures, which meant he should get a move on and finish mending the fences that were supposed to contain them.

Nick relished the idea of hard work, which was sure to get his mind off everything that had happened last night. He still wanted to deck Charlie and hoped that Dani had banished the bastard from her mind and slept peacefully.

Had she made it in to work this morning? Knowing Dani, she probably had. He picked up the phone to find out. She answered right away. "Hi."

"Mornin'. How are you today?"

"Sleepy, but I made it to work. Hey, thanks again for last night. You're the best friend ever."

She assumed they were back to being friends and nothing but. If she only knew that Nick wanted her more than ever. He cleared his throat. "I'm awful glad you're okay."

"You and me both. I told Big Mama what happened."

"You called her at this hour?"

"She's an early riser, so it was a safe bet that she'd be up. Besides, I had to, before she heard from someone else. You know how news spreads around here."

"I sure do. How did she take it?"

"She was upset, but grateful that you showed up. She's going to ban Charlie from the restaurant. Will you call her later, just to make sure she's okay?"

"I was planning on stopping by her place, anyway, to convince her to make an appointment with her doctor."

"I'll keep my fingers crossed. Well, I should go and get things ready."

"If you want anything, call."

As soon as Nick disconnected he blew out a big breath. That had gone well enough. Next, he phoned Big Mama.

"Good morning, my sweet, sweet Nick," she cooed. "Thank you for what you did last night."

Her praise warmed him and also made him uncomfortable. Dani deserved most of the credit for her own efforts at protecting herself. "Dani was amazing. She bit the heck out of Charlie's tongue. I expect he'll be hurting for a while. You'd have been proud of her."

"I am, but I'm just as proud of you. I just wish I hadn't encouraged her to go out with Charlie. He seemed such a decent man. Say, have you eaten yet?"

"Not yet, but I'm getting ready to."

"Come over and let me make you breakfast, as my way of thanking you."

Just the mention of one of Big Mama's breakfasts made his mouth water. During the meal he would talk to her about that doctor's appointment. "Okay. When should I be there?"

"Give me thirty minutes."

The sun hadn't come up yet when he sat down at Big Mama's kitchen table and helped himself to mouth-watering muffins, cheesy scrambled eggs and sausage. Not exactly health food.

Nick eyed Big Mama and had to admit that Dani was right—her skin was pasty, and there was no sign of her usual hearty appetite. Nick was worried. He answered her questions about the night before, then got down to business.

"This is delicious," he said. "But aren't you supposed to cut down on this kind of food?"

The scowl she gave him could have frozen the sun. "You sound like Dani. I'll bet she asked you to talk to me about my health." Before he could answer, she waved her hand dismissively. "I'll tell you what I told her. It's indigestion."

"So why are you eating foods that will make it worse?"

"Because I want to." She raised her chin defiantly, reminding him of Dani. "I want you and Dani to quit worrying about me." She reached in her sweater pocket for a bottle of prescription antacids. "A couple of these will take care of the problem."

Nick didn't believe that. "Humor me, anyway— Call tomorrow and make an appointment with Dr. Adelson."

"Oh, all right. Then will you both stop nagging me?"

Reassured, he smiled. "You have my word on that."

"You look like your regular self," Sly said to Dani when he and Lana entered her apartment late Sunday afternoon.

Dani handed Fluff to her sister-in-law, who cooed and cuddled him like a baby.

"I told you when you called that I'm fine. Instead of dropping Johanna at Lana's parents' for Sunday dinner, you both should have gone, too."

"We wanted to be with you. We'll see them next week." Lana set the cat down. "How was work today?"

"Different." News had traveled even faster than Dani had imagined. Everyone had heard what Charlie had pulled. "Follow me into the kitchen and I'll pour the wine."

"People say that Charlie Schorr's tongue will never be the same," Sly said as they headed down the hall. He squeezed her shoulder with brotherly affection. "You sure know how to take care of yourself."

"You're kind of a celebrity," Lana added. "Everyone's talking about your strong bite."

Dani laughed at that. She was proud that she'd refused to be a victim. She poured them each a glass of wine, and they sat down at the kitchen table. "Customers kept coming up to me and offering sympathy." She made a face. "Do I act like I need people to feel sorry for me?"

"They're just showing that they care," Lana said. "Isn't it wonderful to be loved?"

Dani ran her finger around the stem of her glass. "It is nice that people care, but I'm not used to all the attention."

"What did Big Mama say?" Lana asked.

"She was upset, of course. She's banned Charlie permanently from Big Mama's Café."

"I should hope so. How's she doing? You've been worried about her health."

"She's still dragging herself around and still suffering what she claims is heartburn. She's been saying she'll make a doctor's appointment, but she keeps putting it off. Then this morning Nick went over to her house and talked to her about it. He did what I couldn't—convinced her to call the doctor's office tomorrow morning." Dani was so relieved.

"Nick's good people," Sly said. "After last night, I like him even better than I did before. That reminds me, the March Madness games start Wednesday night. We're having our usual party. This year will be extra fun because the Montana Grizzlies made it to the playoffs. You'll be at our place to watch the game, right?"

"Me, miss the best March Madness party in town?" Dani smiled. "Never. But what does Nick have to do with March Madness?"

Sly grinned. "Because this year, he'll be joining us. Hey, maybe he can swing by and give you a ride."

After last night, Dani's distinctly non-platonic feelings for Nick had upped several notches on the heat scale. Seeing him, and worse, being alone with him in a car, probably wasn't the best idea.

"Um, I don't know," she said carefully.

Sly frowned. "I thought you two were tight."

"We are. It's just… You've never invited him before, and you caught me by surprise. Besides, he lives closer to you than me, and driving all the way over here, then to your place again seems like a total waste of time and gas."

"True." Dani's brother slanted her a look. "Why am I getting the sense you don't want him to come?"

Because I have the hots for him wasn't going to work. While Dani struggled unsuccessfully for a plausible-sounding answer to her brother's question, Lana cut in.

"I'm hungry. How does Thai food sound?"

To Dani's relief, talk of food distracted her brother. As soon as Lana phoned in the order, he grabbed his keys.

"Be back soon." He kissed his wife, grinned at Dani, and left.

"Now, then," Lana said, scrutinizing her curiously. "What exactly did you and Nick do last night?"

Dani explained that Nick had brought his date to Baker's

while she and Charlie were there. "He said he didn't trust Charlie and wanted to keep an eye on me," she went on. "Can you believe that? I don't need a protector. I'm pretty good at taking care of myself."

"You certainly are," Lana said. "You proved that last night. But back to Nick."

"He said that some sixth sense warned him to come over. And I have to admit that when he showed up just after I bit Charlie, I was awful glad."

"I would've been, too. That man cares a lot about you."

Dani knew that. "He was so great about everything. He stayed with me until I calmed down. We had hot cocoa and talked." She smiled at the memory.

She'd also cuddled with him on the couch. Desire had washed over her, but for once, she'd been able to hide her longing from him and preserve their relationship.

"Now our friendship is on track again," she said. "It's a big relief."

"Funny, you don't look or sound at all relieved."

"Actually, I'm pretty confused," Dani admitted. "On the one hand, I'm super glad we're friends again, but on the other hand…" Wondering how to explain, she paused a moment and gathered her thoughts. "Since we kissed a couple weeks ago, I can't help but want an encore. And not just kisses, either. I want a whole lot more."

Lana almost smiled. "You've heard my opinion on that."

"And you know mine—mixing passion with friendship will never work for Nick and me."

Dani valued that friendship more than just about anything. And yet, if Nick had made even one small move to kiss her last night, she would have welcomed him. Which would've undone their friendship all over again. Her seesawing feelings were driving her crazy.

"He believes we're back to being platonic, and when he called early this morning to check on me and relay his success with Big Mama, I played my part. He has no idea how badly I lust for him." She buried her hands in her face and moaned. "I guess I'm saying that I shouldn't see him again until I get him out of my system. That's why I'm hesitant about this March Madness thing."

"Avoiding him won't help your friendship any, especially if he has no idea why. Don't you think you should talk to him?"

"Maybe. The trouble is, whenever I get close to him, all I want to do is kiss him again." It was a wonder he hadn't guessed. "I hoped that dating would help me forget the feelings I have for him. That's why I went out with Charlie, even though I didn't want to. That sure backfired." At the mere mention of the man, Dani grew cold. She pushed Charlie and the awful evening from her mind. "What should I do?"

"I can't answer that, but I will share an observation." Lana gave her a steadfast gaze. "I'm guessing your feelings for Nick are deeper than you realize."

"You're saying I'm falling for him?" No way, none at all. She was not letting herself do that.

"Not falling for him," Lana said. "You've already fallen."

"I haven't! Don't say that! Loving Nick that way would be a complete disaster."

"Hey, I'm just calling it as I see it." Lana spread out both hands. "Are you going to come to our party?"

After the conversation she'd just had with Lana, Dani was more certain than ever that she should steer clear of Nick. She sighed. "Unless I want Sly breathing down my neck, wondering why I'm staying away, I don't think I have a choice. But it'll be hard."

She wasn't sure how she would stay away from Nick, but somehow she had to.

"I can't say what's right for you," Lana said. "Only you can decide that. Just understand that whatever you do, you have my support."

"You're the best sister-in-law ever. I'm tired of talking about my problems. What's new with you?"

Lana got excited. "You remember that Sly and I have been looking into adopting."

"Something's happened already!" Dani guessed.

Her sister-in-law nodded. "We heard from our attorney last Thursday. There's a fifteen-year-old teenage girl in another state who's four months pregnant. She's a top student and she and her boyfriend aren't ready to take on the challenges of parenting. She picked Sly and me as well as two other couples, and asked for a letter explaining why we think we're the best choice to be the parents of her baby. We're working on that now."

"How exciting! If you need a reference, I'm your woman."

"We're not supposed to use letters from family, but our housekeeper—Mrs. Rutland—and several employees and parents from the daycare have offered to write letters for us."

Dani jumped up and hugged her sister-in-law. "I'm so happy for you!"

"It's early days yet, and Sly and I don't want to get our hopes up… We probably won't hear from the girl for a few months."

"Well, you may not want to get too excited, but I have a good feeling about this."

Dani's landline phone rang. "There's Sly with our food." She buzzed him up. "We haven't even set the table yet. You let him in, and I'll pull out plates and silverware. And please, don't say a word to him about Nick."

"I would never betray your confidence." Lana pantomimed locking her lips.

NICK AND HIS crew spent the next few days busting their chops on the fence repairs. By Wednesday night he was ready for some March Madness craziness at Sly and Lana's.

He was looking forward to seeing Dani there and actually talking to her. They hadn't spoken since he'd called to let her know that Big Mama had agreed to make a doctor's appointment, but they'd texted a few brief messages. They were both extra busy.

Dani seemed to have really bought into the back-to-being-friends thing. Nick wasn't there by a long shot, but he'd never let her know that.

Thanks to a minor disaster involving a calf moose stuck in one of the barbwire fences he and his crew had recently mended, he arrived at Sly and Lana's after the game had started.

By the number of vehicles parked in the driveway, he figured there were quite a few people inside. He spotted Dani's sedan. Great, she was here.

Nick rang the doorbell and waited, but no one answered. No doubt, everyone was too wrapped up in the game. The door was unlocked, so he let himself in. In the large entry he removed his denim jacket, then found a hanger in the closet. He noted that the great room across the way was crowded with men and women, most of whom he recognized.

All eyes were on the action on the big screen TV. Nick searched the room for Dani. She was seated on one of the smaller couches beside Lana and Sly. In jeans and a V-neck sweater that clung to her curves, she looked fantastic.

Everyone seemed to notice him at the same time. People called out greetings, and Nick returned them.

"Sorry I'm late," he said. "Had a run-in with a calf moose stuck in a barbwire fence. Her mama didn't appreciate me being there, but eventually I got the baby out."

"You missed a couple of great plays," someone said.

"I listened to some of the game on the drive here. The Grizzlies are pounding their opponents."

"Go, go, go!" a group on the sectional shouted.

Lana gestured him over. "I'm glad you made it." She stood and offered him her seat on the plush leather.

Nick shook his head. "Stay put. I'll grab a chair."

"Don't bother—I want to check on some appetizers in the oven and make sure Johanna didn't kick off her covers. Besides, I've been saving this place for you."

He didn't miss the *are you kidding me* face Dani gave her sister-in-law. Wary now, he sat down beside her. "Hey," he said, keeping his voice low so as not to disturb the others.

"Hi." Dani quickly redirected her attention to the basketball action.

Nick checked the screen. The Grizzlies had called a time-out. "How're you doing?" he asked.

"I'm good."

Avoiding eye contact and holding herself straight so as not to touch him? Sure she was. Maybe she wasn't as comfortable with him as she said. "Has Big Mama met with the doctor yet?" he asked.

Dani finally met his gaze. "She's taking a few hours off tomorrow morning to see him. I'm relieved, but also a little scared."

"Yeah, me, too." Nick put his hand over hers and gave a reassuring squeeze. The way a friend would.

Whether it was the touch or the words he wasn't sure, but she quickly pulled out of his grasp. "I'll let you know how it goes."

The game heated up, and they both trained their attention on that. During halftime, Dani busied herself helping Lana and Sly with the food, and Nick chatted with some of the other guests. When the game restarted, they returned to their seats. The last two quarters were close and wildly exciting. Once or twice Dani started to reach for his hand, but she always stopped herself.

Nick enjoyed the game, but not as much as he should have. He was too confused. What the hell was Dani's problem?

When the Grizzlies won, he knuckle-bumped Sly. Under normal circumstances he would have pulled Dani into a quick hug, but tonight he settled for a high-five.

He waited to talk her until it was time to leave. After thanking Sly and Lana, he grabbed his jacket and followed her outside.

Head down, she hurried off, as if he had the plague and she feared catching it from him. "Wait up, Dani," he called out.

She pivoted toward him. In the harsh light of the motion detector lights, her face was shadowed.

"You're in such a rush that you can't even say goodnight to me?" He frowned. "What the hell is wrong?"

"Nothing, Nick." She dug the toe of her boot into the damp earth. "It's late, and you know how early I have to get up tomorrow. I'm anxious to get home."

Not until they talked. "This won't take long." He tipped up her chin so that he could meet her eyes. "When I left your place Saturday night, I assumed we were okay again. Things seemed all right on the phone and when we texted. But tonight you're sure upset with me."

Dani shook her head. "I'm not, Nick. You're imagining things."

"The hell I am. I know you too well. You barely looked at me tonight. Then you run out the door without a word… Used to be that you'd tell me when something upset you."

She bit her lip, a sure sign he'd hit the mark, and shot a longing glance at her car. "I…I just can't."

A sick feeling settled in Nick's gut. "Is this about Charlie? Has he been bothering you?"

If so, Nick would go after him right now. His hands curled into fists.

"No! Charlie has nothing to do with it, Nick. Can we please save this conversation for later? I really have to get some sleep."

As badly as Nick wanted answers, he couldn't force her to explain. "Whatever." He gave a short, terse nod. "Night."

In a lousy mood, he drove toward the ranch. Things between him and Dani were worse than ever. The hell of it was, this time he was clueless what the problem was, and so had no idea how to fix it.

He was halfway home when his cell rang. Wondering what new ranch emergency had hit, he pulled over to the side of the road and answered without checking the screen. "Kelly here."

"It's me," Dani said.

Wary, Nick closed his eyes. "What's up?"

"I feel terrible about the way we parted."

"Yeah, what was that about?" he asked.

"I don't want to talk about it on the phone. I wasn't

going to say anything ever, in fact, just work things out by myself, but that isn't fair to you. Will you come over?"

What did she mean, *fair?* "When?"

"How about now?"

"See you in a few." Nick disconnected, executed a U-turn and headed toward Dani's.

Chapter Ten

As nervous as a kid on his first date, Nick knocked on Dani's door. But this was no date. Once he understood what her issues were, he could straighten them out.

As long as he didn't bungle this up.

Holding Fluff in her arms, she let him in. "That was fast. How about something to drink?"

Nick shook his head.

"Let's talk in the kitchen," she said, and started forward.

Sitting at the table was probably a good idea. That way they could look straight at each other.

As soon as they were seated Dani cut straight to the chase. "The past few days, I've been doing a lot of soul searching." She paused and fiddled with the cuff of her sweater. "I don't think we should be around each other for a while."

The unexpected words hit like a fist to the gut. Nick winced and blurted, "If you just give me time, I swear, I'll conquer this physical thing I have for you."

She looked surprised. "You were so sweet the other night and tonight, I assumed you already had."

He let out a self-deprecating laugh. "That so called 'sweetness' nearly killed me. For the sake of our friendship I forced myself to behave. Besides, the other night, you were in no shape for what I wanted."

"But I wanted the same thing," she said softly.

The stark desire on her face almost undid him.

"As much as I want us to go back to our purely friendship place, it's impossible," she went on. "Maybe if I could forget those kisses… Unfortunately, I'm not having much luck with that." She glanced away for a moment. "The truth is, my physical, um, feelings for you have only grown stronger."

She lowered her voice to a near whisper, as if confessing something secret and private. "Lately I've been heaving dreams about us. Erotic dreams."

She had no idea what her lowered eyelids and flushed cheeks did to him. The blood in Nick's brain migrated southward, and he was grateful that the table hid his need.

How he itched to pull her close and make those dreams a sizzling reality. But he wasn't that far gone. No matter how bad he wanted Dani, he would hold back. Too much was at stake.

Oblivious of his tortured thoughts, she brushed her hair out of her eyes and went on. "That's why we have to avoid each other for a while, Nick. So that we can both get a grip. It's the only way we'll ever be friends again."

She had a point, but not one Nick wanted to live with. "There is another way," he said.

"I can't imagine what it could be."

"The other night, Sylvie made an interesting comment about our problem."

"What does she have to do with this?" Dani frowned, then looked shocked. "You told her about us. Does she know everything?"

"You mean, the reason I asked her out?" He nodded. "At Baker's, she noticed there was something between you and me. I wasn't going to lie to her. I didn't say much, only that we were trying to stay friends."

"I'll bet she was insulted that you asked her out to forget me," Dani said. "I would be."

"Actually, she was pretty decent about it. Her take was different than ours. She suggested that instead of fighting our attraction to each other, we should explore it and find out where it leads us."

"We both know exactly where it will lead." Dani's eyes were filled with longing and pain. "Having sex will effectively put an end to our friendship. Without that, what are we left with? Sure, we might have great sex, but eventually we'll part ways and stop being friends. I couldn't bear that, Nick."

He was in full agreement. And yet… "Trying to forget we ever kissed hasn't worked," he said. "And going out with someone new was a bust. We could try dating other people again, but right now, I'm just not interested."

"Me, either. After Charlie, I don't even want to date again—not for a while."

For a long moment, neither of them said a word, both lost in their own gloomy thoughts.

Nick finally broke the silence. "You know, Sylvie could be onto something."

Dani opened her mouth, probably to argue, but he held up his hands and she remained silent. "I'm starting to think that getting physical is the only way to get each other out of our systems. Why don't we give in to what we both want?"

"Because I want love and you don't believe you're capable of giving it to me."

"There is that risk." Nick raked his hand through his hair. "As bad as I want you, and lately, making love with you is pretty much all I think about, I sure as hell don't want to lose you."

"This is like being stuck between a rock and a hard place—pure torture." Dani rubbed absently at a water stain on the table. Suddenly she sat up straight. "But… Hold on a sec. If we go into this thing with our eyes open… Yes. Then your plan just might work."

Nick frowned. "You lost me."

"Look at my track record. I expected every one of my boyfriends to love me, so of course, I let myself love them, too. Then when things didn't work out, my heart got broken."

"True."

"But with you, I know the score upfront. You'll never love me. And because I know that, I'll hold on to my heart and—"

"You won't get hurt."

Dani nodded.

"Okay, but how can you be sure you won't fall in love with me?" he asked.

"I just won't."

Nick had his doubts. Not because he was cocky but because they'd been friends for too long. No matter what she said, it could still happen. "What if you do?"

"I won't."

She leaned forward and stared him straight in the eye. That and her firm tone almost convinced him.

"I think we should test out your plan," she said. "At the very least we should kiss again, just to find out if what we felt the last time was a fluke. Are you in?"

Her eager, hungry gaze went straight to his groin, and God help him, he was *all* in.

He laughed, a strangled sound. "You're impossible."

"Maybe I am, but you, Mr. Kelly, are driving me crazy. Now for that test."

She rose and came around to him. With her hip, she shoved the table aside so that she could step between his thighs.

Nick swallowed hard. He pulled her onto his lap and rested his forehead against hers. She was so close, he could see the tiny silvery flecks in her fathomless eyes.

"You sure?" he asked, his voice ragged with need.

Dani twined her arms around his neck, bringing her soft breasts flush against his chest. "Does this answer your question?"

She closed her eyes and pursed her lips just a little, an offering to him.

With a groan, he took.

NICK WAS KISSING HER. At last.

There was no gentleness in his kiss, only raw hunger, as if he were starving and she was food.

Breathing hard, he pulled away. "It definitely wasn't a fluke."

She had to struggle to understand his words. "What?"

"The chemistry that we felt between us before. It's just as strong now."

"I'm not sure," she said. "Maybe we should do another test."

Needing to get closer, she moved so that she was straddling his lap.

"I was mistaken," he murmured several passionate kisses later. "This thing between us—it's even more powerful than it was before."

"I'd have to agree." Dani shifted closer, so that the most sensitive part of her body pressed against the hardest part of his. Dampness flooded her panties, and for a long while, she lost herself in the smell and taste of Nick. When he finally cupped her tingling breasts through her pullover, she melted into a puddle of longing. Soon, touching her through her sweater wasn't enough.

As if reading her mind, he tore his mouth from hers, grasped the hem and pulled the sweater over her head.

Dani wished she'd worn something sexier than a plain beige bra, but Nick didn't seem to mind. With eyes as dark as rich chocolate, he traced her nipple through the fabric. It beaded into a hard point. Dani moaned with pleasure, and he traced the other nipple.

Craving the feel of his hands on her bare skin, she reached behind her, unfastened her bra and let it slip from her body. Cool air whispered over her feverish breasts.

For a few moments, Nick studied her through heavy-lidded eyes. "You're everything I imagined and more," he said. He cupped her in his hot hands and squeezed gently. "Soft and warm, and beautiful."

No other man had ever sounded so awed. For some reason, Dani's eyes filled.

Instantly, Nick let her go. "I hurt you."

"Not at all." She guided him back to her aching breasts.

"Then why the tears?"

"Because…" Dani struggled to put her emotions into words. "Because you think I'm beautiful."

He froze. "Surely I'm not the first man to tell you that."

If she admitted he was, would he find her less attractive? In the end, she gave him the truth. "You're the first."

"Those other guys were blind, then."

Nick unbuttoned his twill shirt and shrugged out of it, exposing broad shoulders and a solid chest honed and defined from years of hard, physical labor. Dani traced the scar on his left shoulder, still red from an incident with barbwire several months ago. "Does it hurt?" she asked.

"Not when you touch it. Let's move to a more comfortable place."

Cupping her bottom in his big hands, he stood and brought her with him. She wasn't exactly little, but he lifted her as if she weighed nothing. She circled his hips with her thighs and pushed her breasts against the smattering of hair on his chest.

Skin to skin. Heaven.

She was almost panting now.

Nick's mouth fused with hers. He took her someplace. Dani was too aroused to know or care where. Then she was lying on her back on the couch, with Nick on top, supporting his weight on his arms. Kissing her with a passion that matched her own.

Leaving her lips, he nibbled the sensitive place below her ear. Kissed the crook of her shoulder. Planted fevered kisses along her collarbone. Then he captured her mouth in another searing kiss.

It wasn't enough. "Touch me, Nick," she whispered, placing his hands on her sensitized breasts.

"This way?"

He thumbed her nipples. Pleasure shot through her, and she let out a moan. "Yes, like that."

Soon his tongue took over. "And this?"

"Dear God, yes."

Groaning, he moved between her thighs and thrust against her. Her already smoldering body went up in flames. If only they were both completely naked. But even wearing panties and jeans, Dani was on the verge of climaxing. She whimpered with need.

Immediately Nick stilled. "You okay?"

"No. I want you, Nick."

His low laugh sent a rush of heated breath over her breasts. "Patience, Dani."

He was tugging at the zipper of her jeans, when abruptly he swore and pulled away. "That's your phone."

She hadn't even heard the ring. "I don't care." She pulled him down for another mind-numbing kiss, but he sat up.

"It's after eleven," he said. "It could be important."

Dazed, she sat up, too. Suddenly shy, she covered her breasts with her arm and headed for the kitchen to retrieve her pullover. Ignoring the bra, she tugged the sweater over her head before answering the phone.

"Hello?"

"Dani? I hope I didn't wake you. It's Jewel."

Dani hadn't spoken with Big Mama's closest friend since she'd last seen her at Big Mama's house weeks ago. Why would she call, and so late?

Warning bells sounded in Dani's head. "No, I'm awake. What's up?"

Nick had followed her and also donned his shirt. For his benefit, she switched her cell phone to speaker mode.

"Your mother came over to my house for dinner and cards tonight. Just as she was getting ready to go home…" Jewel's voice broke. "She was suddenly in a lot of pain, and we feared she was having a heart attack."

"A heart attack?" Oh, dear God. Dani sank onto a kitchen chair. "Hang up and call 9-1-1!"

"I did, honey, right away. We're at the hospital now."

"And you're just getting around to calling me?" Suddenly cold, Dani shivered. "Is she okay?"

"Yes and no."

Impatient, Nick took over. "This is Nick. What's going on, Jewel?"

"Hi, Nick. What are you doing with Dani so late, when she has to get up at four-thirty in the morning?"

No telling what the woman was thinking, but Dani wasn't going to worry about that now. She exchanged a look with Nick.

"Answer the question, Jewel," he said.

"All right. The good news is, Trudy didn't have a heart attack," she replied. "The bad news is, they're keeping her here overnight so that they can watch her. She's going to have surgery tomorrow."

"Surgery," Dani repeated, frowning. "What for?"

"She has a partially blocked artery, and the doctors want to clear it."

Jewel tried to explain further, but Dani couldn't focus. "I'll be right there," she said.

As soon as she disconnected, panic took over. Her eyes filled. "She can't die. Oh, please don't let her die."

"Don't let yourself go there, Dani."

Nick put his arm around her and pulled her comfortingly close. The heat from his body helped warm her very cold insides. Moments later, she hurried to the living room and grabbed her purse.

"My keys… Where are my keys?"

"Check the side pocket of your purse, where you usually keep them. But you won't need them. I'm driving. Let's go."

BEFORE NICK BRAKED the truck to a complete stop in the hospital parking garage, Dani was out the passenger door, hurrying toward the hospital entrance. Just before she reached it, he caught up and snagged her arm. "Slow down, Dani."

"I have to get to Big Mama right away," she said, sounding terrified.

"Another few minutes won't change anything." Fearing she might hyperventilate, Nick massaged her wrists and forced himself to use a relaxed tone at odds with his own tension. "For her sake and yours, calm down."

She gave a jerky nod. "I'll try."

After she pulled in and blew out a few deep breaths, Nick opened the door and they entered the lobby.

Hard to believe that thirty minutes earlier they'd been enjoying the hottest foreplay of his life. Now he wanted only to shield Dani from the pain and worry shadowing her eyes.

With her mother in such bad shape, that was impossible.

In the lobby, he pressed the elevator button for the floor where Jewel had said Big Mama was staying. On the ride up, Dani sucked in several more deep breaths.

"That's much better," he said.

"It doesn't really help. I'm scared, Nick."

As was he. He put his arm around her and kept her close.

God, he hated hospitals, this one in particular. He'd last been here roughly two years earlier, arriving shortly after his father had suffered a heart attack. His father had lingered for a few hours, hanging onto life long enough for Nick and Jamie, and even their mother, to say goodbye.

It wasn't until then, on his deathbed, that he'd finally forgiven Nick's mother for cheating on him. His forgiveness had enabled her to make peace with herself and let go of the guilt that had filled her for years.

"I wish my dad had been as lucky as Big Mama," he said. "If he'd been admitted here before his heart attack, he might still be alive."

"I can't even imagine." Dani bit her lip. "Big Mama

could… The same thing could have happened to her. It still could." She swallowed hard.

"Hey, she's in the cardiac wing, where she'll be carefully monitored," he assured her. "Tomorrow, the surgeon will fix her up as good as new."

"Please let that be true." Dani closed her eyes, her lips moving as if in prayer.

As soon as the elevator door opened, Dani headed out. A few feet away, Jewel stood waiting for them.

As her gaze darted between them with interest, Nick barely suppressed an eye roll. Jewel had never been one to keep things to herself. God only knew what she'd say about him and Dani.

After they greeted each other, Jewel said, "I'm not family so they won't let me visit your mother. But they'll let you in, Dani. Now that you're here, I'm going home to get some sleep. I'll be back in time for her surgery in the morning."

"You saved her life." Dani grasped the older woman's hands in hers. "I don't know how I'll ever be able to thank you."

"No thanks needed, honey."

They embraced, and Jewel left.

At the nurses' station, a kindly nurse filled in Dani and Nick about the next morning's surgery. "It's called balloon angioplasty, and it's scheduled for seven tomorrow morning," she said. "Dr. Cruise will insert a balloon-tipped catheter in the narrowed section of your mother's artery. Then he'll gently inflate the balloon and position a stent that will expand and keep the artery open."

"Is it dangerous?" Dani asked, reaching for Nick's hand.

"Not with Dr. Cruise doing the procedure. He does

one to two of these per month. Your mother will be in expert hands."

"That's a relief. Can I see her?"

The nurse nodded. "Of course, but don't stay long. She's very tired. She needs to rest and stay calm."

Dani tugged on Nick's hand. "Come on."

"Are you a family member?" the nurse asked.

"He's practically family," Dani said. "He's my…" She hesitated a moment, as if she wasn't sure what Nick was to her after those kisses and caresses. "My best friend."

Relieved that after what they'd shared earlier, she still considered him a friend and only a friend, Nick let out the breath he'd been holding.

The nurse glanced at him. "Sir, I'm afraid you'll have to stay in the waiting room."

"Not a problem." Nick let go of Dani's hand. "When you're finished, come find me out here."

She nodded, then pivoted toward her mother's room.

Chapter Eleven

When Dani entered the hospital room, Big Mama was asleep. Not wanting to disturb her, Dani tiptoed toward the bed. The wires attached to her chest and wrists made the normally robust woman look frail.

Dani was already worried, but seeing her mother like this only brought home the danger Big Mama was in.

She felt so powerless. If only Nick was here with her, holding her hand in silent comfort and support. She wished he would offer a lot more than that, but this wasn't the time or place to examine her deepening feelings for him.

Although she didn't intend to stay long, she was too shaken to remain standing. After quietly pulling a chair to the side of the mattress, she sat down. Behind the bed, a machine beeped quietly, an electric sentry keeping watch. She found that oddly comforting. Nick was right—here in the hospital, her mother would be watched over and cared for with the kind of attention only medical experts could give.

The nurse knocked softly on the open door and entered to take her mother's vitals. Dani stood and moved out of the way. She picked up the chair and carefully returned it to its place at the side of the little room.

As soon as the nurse lifted Big Mama's hand to check

her pulse, she awoke. She gave Dani a tired smile. "Jewel must've given you a call. Come here and give your Big Mama a hug."

"As soon as the nurse finishes."

Moments later, the nurse smiled. "Pulse, temperature and numbers are within normal range, Mrs. Alexander. I'll check on you in a few hours." She slipped out.

Dani bent over the hospital bed, gently hugging her mother and furiously blinking back tears. When she pulled away, she forced a smile. "I hear you're having surgery in the morning."

Her mother grimaced. "Like it or not."

"It's a necessity. And I'm guessing that when it's over, you'll feel a lot better."

"I'll find out, won't I? You'll come visit after work tomorrow."

"I wouldn't think of going to the restaurant," Dani said. "I'm going to be right here at the hospital."

"There's no need for that, missy. You ought to be at the restaurant. Otherwise, who'll take care of business?"

"On the drive here, I called Sadie and Mike and put them in charge. I also contacted Colleen and Melanie, and asked them both to fill in." Melanie was a retired waitress who worked on an as-needed basis.

Sick as her mother was, she chided Dani. "You shouldn't use the phone while you drive."

"I wasn't driving—Nick was."

"Oh? Where is he?"

"In the waiting room. The nurse wouldn't let him come in because he isn't family."

"He's *like* family. Give him a hug for me. Now about Big Mama's Café. Sadie and Mike don't know how to run a restaurant."

"They've all worked for you for years," Dani said. "They're experienced enough."

Big Mama closed her eyes. "I'm too tired to care. Thursdays are pretty slow these days, so I guess they'll manage all right. Go on home now and get some sleep."

"Are you sure you want me to leave? I could ask for a cot and stay with you all night."

"That would just keep me awake. Go."

"All right." Dani kissed her mother's gray-tinged cheek. "I'll be back in a few hours. If you need me for anything before then, have the nurse call."

IN NO TIME, Dani was in Nick's truck again, listening to country Western music while he drove through the darkness toward her apartment building.

Over the last few hours the temperatures had dropped to below freezing, and Nick had cranked the heat up nice and high.

Warm and exhausted, Dani finally let down. "I hate that she has to have surgery in the morning, but you were right—it's a relief that she's spending the night in the hospital."

"A big load off your shoulders, huh."

She nodded. "Now I understand a little of what you went through." She had no idea how she would even cope if Big Mama had died.

"I wouldn't wish that on my worst enemy." Nick yawned. "What did your mom say when you walked into her room?"

"That I should go to work tomorrow and come to the hospital after the restaurant closed." Dani snorted.

"That's Big Mama for you."

"Have you spoken with your mom lately?" she asked,

wanting to talk about something else. "Is she getting excited about the wedding?"

"I guess. She wanted me to remind you that it's set for the first Friday in May, at three o'clock."

"Let her know that it's already on my calendar."

They chatted a few more minutes before slipping into comfortable silence.

Dani's eyes drifted shut. When she opened them again, Nick was pulling into the apartment complex.

"Did you have a nice nap?" he teased.

"Actually, I did." Groggy, she stretched. "Thanks for being there tonight, Nick."

"I wouldn't choose to be anywhere else." He pulled up to the front door and let the engine idle. "The surgery's at seven tomorrow morning. I'll pick you up at six."

She shook her head. "This is a busy season for you, and you have a lot to do. Let's meet at the hospital instead. Then you can leave if you have to."

He didn't argue. "Sweet dreams." He touched her cheek, but made no move to kiss her, even on the cheek.

The delicious kisses and caresses they'd shared only hours ago seemed unreal, from another lifetime. But Dani's feelings for Nick were totally here and now.

They went deeper than friendship. A whole lot deeper. And they would never be returned.

The second she let herself into her apartment, Fluff came running.

"It's been a rough few hours," she said as he followed her to the bedroom. "But Big Mama's going to be okay, and that's what really matters."

She readied herself for bed and climbed in gratefully. Yet as tired as she was, she didn't fall asleep right away. Fluff snuggled against her, and she curled her fingers in his thick fur. Soon his loud purrs filled the silence.

"I may have really screwed up tonight," she admitted in the dark. "No matter what I told Nick, I think I'm falling for him."

She should put the brakes on and stop things before they went any further and she got hurt. But she wanted Nick more than she'd ever wanted a man. And they'd agreed earlier that there was only one way to put out that fire—to make love. All she had to do was keep her heart out of it and she'd be okay.

Oh, *that* would be easy. She groaned. "No matter what, we can't let him know. Then our friendship will go south, fast. Got that?"

The cat didn't seem to care. He was too busy purring and batting her hand for more attention.

AFTER ALL OF four hours' sleep, Nick returned to the hospital. Now he was seated with Dani and Jewel in the waiting room outside the cardiac surgery area. At 6:00 a.m., they were among a handful of people who had family members facing early morning surgery.

Nick had bought both women coffees from the cafeteria. Jewel had quickly drained her cup. Dani, who claimed she couldn't function without the stuff, left hers untouched on the end table next to her chair. For once, her expression was difficult to read, but the way she curled and uncurled a scrap of paper around her index finger spoke volumes.

She'd already lost both her birth parents. She couldn't lose Big Mama, too. An ache filled Nick's chest. He put his arm around her shoulders and kept it there, ignoring the speculative purse of Jewel's lips. Let her talk.

Pretending a calm he didn't feel, he stretched out his legs, tipped his head back against the wall and closed his eyes. According to the nurse, Big Mama's surgery was supposed to be a piece of cake, but he wasn't at all sure she'd pull through. He wasn't a praying man, but he prayed now for the life of the woman who'd taken Dani in as her own, and who meant so much to him.

"A few years ago, a cousin of mine had balloon angioplasty," Jewel said. "She breezed right through it. I'm sure Trudy will do the same."

Dani crossed the fingers of both hands and held them up before again toying with the paper scrap. "Big Mama has felt lousy for weeks. She was scheduled to see Dr. Adelson this morning. I just wish… She almost had a heart attack last night! Why didn't she make her appointment sooner? If it wasn't for you, Nick, she would have continued to put it off. I should have pushed her harder to go in right away."

Nick remembered a similar guilty feeling—that if only he'd done something to make his father seek medical advice, he might not have suffered his heart attack.

"As if either of you could budge her," Jewel said. "We all know that no one can push Trudy Alexander to do anything she doesn't want to do."

The same thing had applied to Nick, Senior, which had been pointed out to Nick numerous times. He'd never quite believed it, though. For two long years he'd blamed himself.

Now, watching Dani suffering through the same thing, reality sank in. It wasn't his fault that his father had died.

A weight he hadn't realized he'd carried fell from his shoulders.

"Jewel is right," he said. "No one can force another person to do what they don't want to do."

"I guess not," Dani conceded. "But I wish I understood why she put off scheduling the appointment."

"Because she assumed she was suffering a bad case of indigestion." Jewel tsked.

"Or maybe she was scared," Nick guessed.

The door labeled Medical Staff Only opened and Dr. Cruise, a tall, fiftysomething male in scrubs and a cap, strode through. He'd introduced himself before the surgery. As he headed toward them, they all stood up.

"The surgery went well and the stent is in place," he said.

"Oh, thank God." Dani sagged against Nick. Equally relieved, he tightened his arm around her.

"What happens next?" she asked.

"We'll be keeping her in the hospital for a few days. When she goes home, she'll need to take it easy for several weeks, until she heals."

"When can I see her?" Dani asked.

"She's weak and groggy right now, but you can visit for a few minutes."

"I don't suppose Nick and I can go in with Dani?" Jewel asked.

"Not today, but probably tomorrow. Call first to make sure."

"All right." Jewel sighed. "I may as well go home, then. Let her know I love her."

"You go ahead, too, Nick," Dani said.

Needing to get back to the ranch, he nodded. "I'll check in with you later. Let your mom know that I'll stop by and see her tomorrow."

AFTER A LONG day at the hospital, Dani returned again Friday morning. Jewel showed up, too. People called Dani's cell nonstop, wanting information about Big Mama. After updating her family, Nick and a few close friends, Dani changed her voice mail message. "Big Mama is doing well," it said. "If you're interested in visiting, contact the nurses' station first to get the okay." Then she switched off her phone.

While her mother napped, she and Jewel sat quietly in matching orange vinyl chairs, Jewel working on the cardigan she was knitting for Big Mama, and Dani attempting to read a romance novel that had been in her to-be-read pile forever. Although the book was excellent, Dani was acutely tuned into her mother's every move and sound, and had trouble focusing on the story.

Big Mama woke up and within moments was glaring at Dani. "Quit hovering over me. You did it while I slept and you're doing it now."

To be that bossy, she must be feeling pretty good. Dani exchanged a glance with Jewel, who raised her eyebrows and smiled.

"How can she hover when she's sitting in a chair?" Jewel asked.

"She just is, and stay out of this, Jewel. You're hovering, too. You should go down to the cafeteria and get yourself something to eat, and Dani should be at the restaurant, making sure everything is running smoothly."

Under normal circumstances, Dani would have agreed. But with her mother in the hospital, she couldn't leave. "I trust Sadie and Mike," she said.

"Up to a point. Fridays can be busy, and they need someone to answer to. If it can't be me, it ought to be you."

Dani crossed her arms. "I'm not leaving you."

"Baloney. Sitting around here making small talk is no way to spend a morning. I'm so bored that I'm ready for another nap. Go on, get out of here. Both of you."

"The drill sergeant has spoken," Jewel quipped. "I'm making decent progress on your sweater, Trudy, and I can just as well do it here as at home. But I'm hungry so I'll take your suggestion and go down to the cafeteria and get myself some breakfast."

"Could you sneak me up a muffin?" Big Mama asked, with a hopeful expression. "Chocolate chip, if they have it."

Dani shook her finger. "No more of that for you. From now on, you're following the diet the nutritionist is preparing for you."

"Now who's the drill sergeant," Big Mama said, but she didn't argue further.

Jewel stood. "I'll be back in a little while, Trudy. Dani, I'll touch base with you later."

As soon as she left, Big Mama crooked her finger and beckoned Dani closer. "What is it?" Dani asked.

"Jewel told me that Nick was with you when she called at eleven the other night. She also said he had his hands all over you while I was in surgery." She gave Dani a sly smile.

Dani was going to kill Jewel. "He did not! We're best friends. His arm was around me because I needed him. As for the other night, we both happened to be at Sly and Lana's for March Madness."

No point in enlightening her mother that Nick had actually been at her place when Jewel's call had come in.

"When you get so huffy about it, I can't help but wonder whether you and Nick are more than friends."

Her mother's words surprised her. How had she guessed?

"Well, stop wondering," Dani said. "We're the same as we always have been."

Big Mama ignored her. "I've always secretly hoped the two of you would realize that you were made for each other. What a fine couple you'd make."

She was wrong about that. They would never be a couple. Nick didn't want the same things Dani wanted. "That's never going to happen," she said. "Now please, drop it."

"All right," Big Mama replied, but her eyes held an unconvinced gleam. "I'm tired again. Leave." She closed her eyes.

"Maybe I should stay."

Her mother cracked one eye open. "What part of 'leave' don't you understand?" She made a "shoo" gesture. "Get out of here and go to work."

It was clear that she wanted Dani gone, and maybe that was for the best. Big Mama would be unable to work for at least six weeks. This was Dani's chance to prove that she could run the restaurant for an extended period of time. She may as well start today.

"All right, I'm going." She stood and kissed her mother's cheek. "I'll be back after we close and I catch up on the paperwork."

Chapter Twelve

To Dani's surprise, Big Mama's Café was packed that Friday morning—busier than it had been in ages. As she walked toward Shelby, a hush settled over the room.

"Thank heavens you're here," Shelby said in a low voice. "It's been crazy, like the old days. Sadie, Colleen and Melanie are running themselves ragged."

Dani barely had a moment to wonder at this before Jackson Martin, a retired cattle auctioneer and breakfast regular, called out. "How's your mother, Dani?"

Other diners echoed versions of the same question.

They were here because they cared about Big Mama. Overwhelmed, Dani placed her hand over her heart. "I appreciate your concern, and so will my mother. She'll be in the hospital for a few more days, but she's going to be okay."

A collective sigh of relief filled the room.

"Will she be coming back to work, or is she going to retire?" asked Carol Cook, who did Big Mama's hair at the beauty salon down the block.

"I doubt she's ready to retire just yet," Dani said.

"Show her the card," someone else said.

Shelby pulled a giant card from behind the hostess desk that had to be three feet tall. "It's from all of us," she said. "We're inviting everyone who comes in today to sign it."

For a moment, Dani was speechless. When she recovered herself, she said, "Thank you all so much. Big Mama's going to love this."

After lunch the crowd thinned considerably and Dani sent Melanie and Colleen home. By the time she locked the door at two o'clock, Big Mama's Café was empty.

Leaving Sadie to finish readying the restaurant for the next day, Dani grabbed the two-day stack of mail and headed for the office.

She sat down at her mother's desk and, as usual, sorted everything into piles—catalogues, bills, miscellaneous. An envelope from the bank caught her eye. The monthly statement wasn't due for a week or so, and this didn't look like an ad. Curious, she opened it.

The single sheet of paper was a notification that the restaurant's checking account was overdrawn and listed the hefty fee charged for covering a business overdraft. Dani frowned. Big Mama had always been meticulous about balancing the checking account. She would never let it go into the red. Surely the bank had made a mistake.

Her mother kept the drawer containing the checkbook and ledger locked, but Dani knew where she hid the key. Within moments, she was studying the ledger. The balance in the restaurant's checking account actually *had* dipped below zero.

What the heck? Dani unlocked the filing cabinet and pulled out the bank statements for the past year. To her shock, almost every month, the account had incurred overdraft charges.

Abruptly, Dani sat back. She felt sick to her stomach, and not just because the restaurant was in such a shaky financial condition. It was bad enough that her mother didn't trust her to run the restaurant. That was wrapped in her control issues. But this… Hiding something so serious from her own daughter was far worse.

Dani couldn't help but to view it as a betrayal, one with which she was all-too familiar. The kind that happened when someone she loved and trusted completely broke that trust.

This latest betrayal, like an old, unwanted companion, hollowed out her heart with a pain worse than any breakup she'd ever experienced.

The resulting empty feeling took Dani straight back to that first breach of trust. She'd been four years old, and devastated by her mother's death from cancer. Underneath the loneliness and anguish, an unspoken question smoldered.

How could her mother, who she loved and leaned on completely and without question, leave her?

Of course, her mother hadn't wanted to die, but to Dani's four-year-old mind that was a betrayal.

Two years later, her father had followed her mother into the grave—another betrayal. Then the uncle who took in Sly and Seth had rejected her.

Betrayal after betrayal. From the time Dani had entered the foster care system, she'd worked with a social worker. Thanks to years of therapy, she'd come to understand that most of what had happened in her life was simple bad luck, and had nothing to do with her. She'd accepted this and believed she'd put it all behind her.

Now she realized she hadn't.

As she fought to shake off the pain and anger, the office phone rang, jerking her into the here and now. She actually jumped in her chair, banging her funny bone hard.

"Ouch!" she cried.

What a mess she was.

In no mood to talk to anyone, she considered ignoring the phone. But this was the restaurant line. Rubbing her elbow, she picked up. "Big Mama's Café, Dani speaking."

"You don't sound so good."

Nick's voice was a balm to her heart. At least he hadn't let her down. The hurt receded a little. "I just hit my funny bone," she said. "And it's been kind of a bad day."

"That sucks. I tried your cell phone, but it went straight to voice mail."

"I was getting so many calls about Big Mama this morning that I switched it off at the hospital. You just reminded me that I forgot to turn it back on. How did you know where to find me?"

"I just got home from visiting your mom."

For some reason, the thought of Nick sitting with her mother caused the pain to bloom again. "Oh?" Dani said.

"Yep. She looks much better than when I saw her a few days ago. She says she might get to go home soon."

"We hope it will be next week, but that's up to the medical staff."

This was great news, but Dani realized that it created another problem. Big Mama would need someone to take care of her for a few weeks. With the restaurant to run, Dani couldn't volunteer. She would have to hire someone to come in, even though Big Mama staunchly refused to admit that was necessary. Before Dani had opened the bank notice, she'd assumed her mother would be able to pay for whatever Medicare didn't cover. Now with her money problems, the whole thing was up in the air. But Dani would have to worry about that later.

"When I visited her this morning, she was well enough to boss me around," she said. "She ordered me to come to the restaurant."

"That's a positive sign. She bossed me around, too. I brought her flowers, and she said I shouldn't have wasted the money."

"Huh."

"That was supposed to make you laugh."

As raw as she felt just now, how could she possibly laugh?

At least now she understood why her mother was against making any changes to the restaurant. Changes cost money, and there was none.

"Dani? You still there?"

In an effort to avert a looming headache, she massaged her temples. "I'm here."

"Something's bothering you," Nick said. He knew her too well. "Look, if this is about us and what happened the other night…"

The very mention of those kisses and caresses warmed her. She smiled. "I wanted it, Nick."

"Me, too. I enjoyed what we did."

"So did I."

The silence that fell between them was thick with unspoken feeling. "I want to be with you tonight," he said.

"Come over."

His low growl of approval shot a bolt of heat through her. Grateful for the hunger that drowned out her pain, she closed her eyes.

Then and there, she decided to fill Nick in on Big Mama's money troubles. She needed his input. Needed him, period.

Although the door was closed and no one could hear, Dani lowered her voice. "You asked why I'm upset. Well, I just found out about something…" At a loss how to describe what she'd uncovered, she paused. "Something interesting."

"Yeah?"

"I can't talk about it on the phone, though. I'll explain when we're together."

"You've got me really curious. Text when you leave the hospital tonight, and I'll come right over."

As upset as Dani was with her mother, she was in no mood to face her later. Delivering the big get-well card could wait. She would call and plead work, fatigue and a headache—all very real.

"There's a lot to do here," she said. "So I won't be making another trip to the hospital tonight. Come over anytime after dinner."

CURIOUS ABOUT DANI'S "something interesting" and looking forward to the rest of their evening together, Nick rang her to buzz him in shortly after seven.

A few minutes later, she opened her door to him.

"The rain is really coming down out there," he said, closing it behind him. "Did you hear the thunder?"

Dani nodded. "There's lightning, too. I've been watching out the window. I heard a weather alert that it will continue for a couple of days. I wish it would clear up."

"Yeah. That cat of yours is probably hiding someplace."

Her usual *let's indulge Fluff* grin was absent. "He's under the couch."

Shadows filled her eyes, and her features were drawn and tense. She was in bad shape, as shaken as she'd been the night Jewel had called and broken the news that Big Mama was in the hospital.

Nick's heart contracted in his chest. "Something happened to your mom."

The statement elicited a bitter smile. "She's doing just fine, getting better every day. But you know that."

"Well, something's got you rattled."

"Understatement of the year." Dani flopped onto the couch.

As soon as Nick tossed his jacket aside, he joined her.

She tugged on the cuff of her pullover sweater. "I'm not sure what to do about her. I could sure use some advice."

He was used to this. Dani often sought his advice on her relationship troubles. Not that she ever took it. "Fire away."

"You know that Big Mama refuses to let me pay the bills for the restaurant or so much as let me peek at the checkbook." She fiddled with her sleeve again.

So that's what had her so worked up. "This is the right time to ask her to add you to the account as a co-owner, and also to grant you power of attorney in case something happens to her. That way if you need to, you'll be able to access the funds for payroll and bills. Don't let her put it off. Remind her what happened after my father's heart attack—no one could get into his bank account. It was a big mess."

"Those are good ideas, Nick, but not why I'm upset. Hey, do you want a beer or a pop?" she asked, as if just now realizing she'd forgotten to ask.

"Nah, I'm fine."

She nodded.

"If you're not careful, you'll wear out that sleeve. Spit it out, Dani. What's wrong?"

With a sigh she placed her hands in her lap. "Just before you called this afternoon, I opened a letter from the bank. The business checking account is overdrawn. Of course, after I made today's deposit that's no longer the case. But we were charged a hefty overdraft fee. In the past, Big Mama always kept the checkbook balanced."

"Now and then, everyone overdraws their bank account. I've been there once or twice myself. It sucks, but it's not worth tying yourself in knots."

She gave him a frustrated look. "This isn't some one-time fluke, Nick. I checked the bank statements going back a full year. It's been happening once or twice, almost every month."

"Big Mama always makes payroll, though, right?"

"Since no one has complained about getting a bounced paycheck, she must be. I assume the rest of the bills are also current. Otherwise we wouldn't have electricity or be able to order the food and supplies we need."

"That's a relief. Yeah, the bank balance is a worry—but it isn't really a surprise. You'd be the first to admit that business *has* been falling off."

"That isn't the point! I'm Big Mama's daughter, Nick. Her only family. Yet she doesn't trust me enough to share this with me? If the notice from the bank had arrived on a day when she was at the restaurant, I would never have known."

It was strange, all right, and not good. "You definitely ought to talk with her about this."

"No, *she* should bring it up with *me,* but she never will. What am I supposed to say—that I'm furious with her for not trusting me enough to let me in on how bad things are?" Dani glared at him, and he understood that she was picturing her mother. "She's healing from heart surgery. She's supposed to stay calm."

"I doubt this has anything to do with her trusting you, Dani."

"Oh, no?" Her face contorted in pain, and he realized he'd hit a nerve. "Then why would she keep something so important from me? I can't believe she did that."

Nick had no answers, but he hated seeing Dani hurt. "She probably didn't want to upset you."

Her laugh lacked any humor. "Well, that sure worked."

"I hear you, Dani, but you're making this bigger than it is."

"It's big to me. Huge."

At a loss what to say, Nick tucked her hair behind her ears. "You're her daughter. She loves you."

Her gaze skittered away from his. "She has a funny way of showing it."

This kind of talk was new to him. It was almost as if she doubted Big Mama's love. "You two really need to have a conversation about this," Nick repeated.

"I can't."

"You can. I've seen you do it a hundred times."

"This is different."

Nick frowned. "How so?"

"When two people trust each other, it's easy to disagree or argue because you know that no matter what, you're there for each other."

"Like us." He nodded. "It's the same with you and your mom."

"I used to believe that, but now I'm not so sure. If she doesn't trust me enough to confide in me about the financial situation of the business I've been a part of for years, a business that's supposed to be mine someday, then she doesn't trust me, period."

"I'm not following."

Dani was quiet a moment, thinking. "It's like this," she said. "I've always trusted her completely. Sure there are certain things I don't tell her because some things are private." Her eyes met his, and Nick knew she was remembering what they'd started the other night.

"But she's in on the really important stuff," Dani continued. "That's what families do—talk about the things that matter. Finding out that she's keeping our restaurant's financial problems from me only proves that my trust is one-sided. It feels like a betrayal, Nick. And I can't help but wonder what else she's hiding from me."

Dani chafed her arms as if she were cold. Seconds ticked by before she spoke again. "Say something, Nick."

"What do you mean, 'betrayal?'" he asked.

"If I tell you, you'll think I'm crazy."

"We're best friends, Dani. Nothing you say will change that."

She let out a strangled laugh. "But I'm such a basket case."

"I've always appreciated your basket case moments," he teased.

Biting her lip, she searched his face. Whatever she found there seemed to reassure her. She nodded and exhaled heavily.

"When I found out about the bank account? The hurt I felt reminded me of when I was little and my mom died. And then my dad." She hugged her waist. "Most of the people I really care about have left me."

Her pain was obvious. Nick squeezed her shoulder in sympathy, and thought about his own childhood. "In a way, I can relate," he said. "I was older than you when I lost my parents, although they didn't die. But they were so caught up in their own crap that they more or less withdrew from my life. I could've run away and I'm not sure they'd have noticed. After they divorced it was even worse. Why do you think I ate dinner with you and Big Mama so often?"

Dani's brow wrinkled, and she gave him a sideways look. "You've never mentioned this before."

"You never said you felt betrayed when your parents

died. I guess there are still some things we don't know about each other."

Amazed at that, he played idly with a lock of her silky hair, letting it fall through his fingers. "You're lucky, Dani. Big Mama wanted you so much that she adopted you. You're her daughter and she really does love you."

She let out a sigh. "I suppose I should talk to her. But right now I'm so upset that I'm not sure I can face her by myself." She hesitated and studied her nails for a moment, before meeting his eyes. "Will you be there with me?"

She'd always been so proud of her independence. Sure, now and then she asked him for advice, but she'd never allowed him to get involved in her relationship with Big Mama.

"I don't want you to say anything," she added. "Just be in the room when I talk to her."

"I can do that. When?"

"Definitely while she's in the hospital. That way she won't be able to make too much of a scene. She's supposed to be going home Monday, so it'll have to be either tomorrow or Sunday. How about late tomorrow afternoon, after the restaurant closes and your day winds down?"

Nick nodded. "Works for me."

"We can meet at the hospital. I'll text you when I'm on my way."

"Sounds like a plan."

"Thanks, Nick. Sometimes…I don't know what I'd do without you."

"Back at ya."

But Dani's soft, loving expression worried him. He hoped she wasn't falling for him.

"This is what friends are for," he said to remind her

that the physical attraction between them could never make their relationship any deeper than it already was.

"And you are a dear friend." She smiled at him. "The best."

That was better. Relieved, Nick grinned back.

Their gazes locked. And bam, everything shifted.

The color of her eyes changed from silvery-blue to burnished silver. The color of her desire. Her lips parted slightly, a silent supplication for his kiss.

Hunger for her steamrollered through him. Needing to touch her, to give her the kiss she wanted and a whole lot more, he tipped up her chin. "Dani—"

"Shh." She laid her finger against his lips. "We've done enough talking for now."

She reached for him.

Chapter Thirteen

With a sigh, Dani gave herself over to Nick. No matter what, he would always be there for her. She loved him for that.

Loved him, period.

No, she didn't. *Did not.* Down that road lay certain heartache and loneliness.

He pulled away to press his sexy mouth on the sensitive place just below her ear and she forgot about everything but being with him, here and now.

"I'm going to make love to you tonight," he murmured against the crook of her shoulder.

Each movement of his lips sent delicious sensations through her.

"I'm so ready." Her bedroom was too far away so she tried to pull him down right where they were.

"Not on the couch. In your bed. Come on." He clasped her hand and pulled her to her feet.

On the short walk down the hall, they stopped to share searing kisses that left her breathless, hungry for more and damp between her legs. She lost her sweater and Nick shed his shirt. By the time they reached the bedroom, she was about to go up in flames.

The rain beat furiously against the bedroom windows. Nick flipped on the bedside reading lamp, while Dani pulled the curtains. Facing each other, they slowly finished undressing. Shoes and socks, jeans, until they stood in their underwear. Dani wasn't wearing plain beige this time. She hoped Nick liked her favorite lavender lace bra and matching bikini panties.

But at the moment, she was too busy looking her fill at the man she wasn't supposed to fall in love with to worry about her underwear. Long, lean and muscled, he wore gray boxers. And he was aroused. Because of her.

But it was the tender expression in his eyes that melted her heart. He might not love her, but he cared a lot for her. He trusted her as no one else did. And she trusted him. He would never let her down.

Who was she kidding? She was *head over heels, consequences be damned* in love with Nick.

If he found out, he would cut and run. If she were smart, so would she. But she was too far gone to stop what had been set in motion with that first sizzling kiss all those weeks ago. She needed to make love with him the way she needed her next breath.

Her only salvation was to keep her feelings a secret. Then everything would be fine.

Nick made a slow, heavy-lidded perusal down and up her body. "As much as I like that pretty underwear, it has to go."

With her gaze fastened on his, Dani unhooked the front clasp of her bra and let it slip from her body. His dark chocolate eyes glittered with desire.

As she stepped out of her bikini underwear, he removed his boxers. He was well-endowed and gloriously erect. Dani wanted him so badly. She swallowed.

The corners of his mouth lifted in a smile—he was well aware of his effect on a woman. But the smile faded as his heated gaze returned to her.

"You're perfect," he said in a voice husky with emotion.

Dani knew she wasn't. "No, I'm not. I'm at least fifteen pounds overweight."

"Dani, Dani, Dani, what am I going to do with you? Look in the mirror and see yourself through my eyes."

He pivoted her around so that they faced the full-length mirror that hung on her bedroom door. Stepping behind her, he wrapped his arms around her waist.

Even in the cool spring weather he was sun-bronzed, and his arms were dark next to her pale skin.

She wanted to turn away from her reflection, but he held her where she was. His big, warm palm splayed across her stomach. She considered sucking it in, but changed her mind. She would do as Nick asked, and study herself.

He met her gaze in the mirror. "What do you see, Dani?"

"I see…" The man who owned her heart, holding her tenderly. "I see a handsome cowboy."

"Holding a goddess. Big, round breasts."

With his forefinger, he traced her areola. Pleasure rolled through her, settling in her lower belly. She wanted to close her eyes, but instead stared at her own nipple as it contracted and stiffened. It happened again on the other breast. Watching herself and Nick together in the mirror was the most erotic thing Dani had ever seen.

He clasped her hips. "Curvy hips," he went on, his voice velvety and rich. "Great legs. And the sweetest behind in Montana." He pulled her hard against his erection and nipped the crook of her neck.

Dani moaned. "You're right, Nick, I am beautiful. And so are you."

Wanting him as she'd never wanted a man before, she

angled her head up to kiss him. This time he allowed her to pivot around. Wrapping her arms around his neck, she pulled him down for a deep, passionate kiss.

When it ended, they were both breathing hard. "What do you like, Nick?" she whispered. "Tell me how to please you."

"Tonight isn't about pleasing me, Dani. It's about you and what you want."

Not one of her previous lovers had ever asked or offered to put her first. Her melting heart expanded, until she was lit up from the inside. "I want you to make love with me, Nick."

"That would be my greatest pleasure." Still kissing her, he walked her toward the bed.

In anticipation of tonight, she'd already removed the spread and turned down the covers.

She wanted to lie down, but Nick kept her upright. "Now what, Dani?"

"Kiss me."

"Where?"

"My mouth."

She lost herself in a long, deep kiss that she never wanted to end.

All too soon, Nick broke away. "Now where?"

"My breasts—the nipples."

He took forever getting there, stopping to plant kisses on her neck and shoulders along the way. But then... The first flick of his tongue across her nipple sent heat spiraling through her. Her bones seemed to dissolve, and she was glad to be on the bed.

Later, when she was restless with need and arching up, he raised his head. "Where else?"

She could barely form words. "Everywhere, Nick."

He complied. Each touch and lick was heaven—and

torture. The problem was, he was taking too long. Impatient, she grabbed hold of his ears until he was forced to glance at her.

"Lower," she said.

"Here?" His tongue dipped into her navel.

"That's nice, but even lower."

He continued to tease her until finally he put his mouth where she most wanted him. Seconds later, Dani climaxed.

When she floated back to earth, Nick was grinning. "That was amazing to watch."

"Oh, yeah? Your turn. On your back, Mr. Kelly." As big and strong as he was, he allowed her to push him down. "I hope you brought condoms."

"One or two." He gave her a wicked grin. "Hang on, and I'll get them."

He started to roll to his side, but she stopped him. "Just tell me where they are."

"Yes, ma'am, Miz Pettit. Right hip pocket of my jeans."

"Don't move a muscle."

Dani found several foil packets. She tossed all but one onto the bedside table.

Following her instructions, Nick hadn't moved. Feeling wicked and wild, she straddled him. She opened the packet, extracted the condom and started to roll it on. Nick gritted his teeth.

Dani hesitated. "Am I doing it wrong?"

"You're doing it so right that I'm about to go over the edge. I'm not letting that happen without you." He removed her hand and sheathed himself.

Then he pulled her down on top of him. As sated as she'd been moments ago, she wanted him again.

A moment later, poised above him, she lowered herself

slowly down, until she was exactly where she wanted to be—intimately joined with Nick.

He groaned.

"Do you like that, Mr. Kelly?"

"I do."

She began to move. Slowly at first, then faster, until heat and need took control of every cell in her body. She was on the verge of letting go when Nick moved his hand between them and thumbed her most sensitive place.

For the second time, Dani shattered. He swiftly followed.

Later, when her heart had slowed from warp speed to normal, she found herself cuddled against his chest.

He kissed the top of her head. "How are you doing?"

Dani ached to confess that she loved him, but that would ruin everything. She propped herself up on her elbow and gave him a bright smile. "Good. *Really* good. I really enjoyed focusing on my pleasure. You?"

Nick's grin was pure male satisfaction. Outside, thunder rumbled so hard, it shook the windows. Despite the curtains, the lightning that followed was clearly visible.

"I enjoyed pleasing you," he said. "And you—you blew me away." He reached over and flipped out the light.

His easy reaction reassured her that he had no idea that he owned her heart, lock stock and barrel. Drowsy, content and secure that her secret was safe, she closed her eyes.

Her last thought was that she should put herself first more often.

Lying on his back beside Dani, his head propped on his arms, Nick stared into the darkness. She lay curled against his side, sleeping as only a thoroughly sated woman can. The sex had been fantastic, the best he'd ever experienced, and he should've been asleep, too.

Or waking her for more.

His body approved of that idea and began to stir. But instead of allowing his hunger to lead him, Nick hesitated. Tonight had been unforgettable, and not just because of the sex. Dani had been through a lot. Revealing the deep, childhood wounds she still carried took courage and trust.

As raw and vulnerable as she'd been, making love with her probably hadn't been the smartest move. He should have stopped while he still could. But Dani had wanted to make love as bad as him, and she'd been impossible to resist.

In the throes of passion, she was something special— her skin flushed and her head thrown back. Pleasuring her had been a real turn-on.

But after… The pure joy shining in her sweet smile, the soft, trusting glow in her eyes… Nick had realized exactly what she felt for him.

Love.

Dani had fallen for him.

She'd promised she wouldn't, but he knew how it was with her, had figured she wouldn't be able to keep this particular promise.

And yet he'd gone ahead and let his desire drown out his common sense.

Calling himself every bad name in the book, he silently swore and wished to God that he could travel back in time, to the night he'd first kissed her, and undo it. Then he wouldn't be in this mess.

Too late now.

The ceaseless rain pummeled the window, and a burst of thunder shook the air, as if Mother Nature herself was angry with him. Lightning flashed, so bright it lit up the room despite the curtains. Too close for comfort.

Murmuring something unintelligible, Dani burrowed closer. Feeling fiercely protective of her, Nick pulled the covers up over her shoulders and brushed her hair out of her face. Tenderness washed over him, and his chest expanded with emotions he didn't understand.

They scared him.

Dani had been hurt too often—she'd reminded him of that earlier tonight. He didn't want his name added to the list of people who'd let her down. That was the source of his fear, he assured himself.

Because no matter how badly he wanted to avoid hurting her, and he wanted that more than anything, he would not be like his father, wouldn't let Dani or any other woman sidetrack him from his goals of making the ranch profitable. He would never fall in love.

Dread for the morning ahead filled him. Waking up beside Dani, bearing the full light of those love-filled eyes…

Nick itched to get up and leave *now,* but he wasn't about to walk out on her while she was sleeping. He might be a dog, but he wasn't that low.

There had to be a way out of this while still keeping the friendship intact. But for the life of him, he didn't know what it was.

"Wake up, Dani. It's almost four-thirty."

Groggy, Dani opened her eyes. Light from the hallway spilled into the room. "Did the alarm go off already?" she mumbled. "I didn't hear it."

"I turned it off when I got up." Instead of lying next to her, Nick was standing by the bed. Fully dressed.

"You can't leave without breakfast," she said, pulling the covers with her as she sat up.

"I have to. Everyone but Blake and Wally has the day off, and there's a lot to do."

"None of the coffee places are open yet. At least let me make you a cup. You can take one of my thermoses." She flipped on the reading lamp, blinking in the sudden brightness.

"I don't have time to wait."

Dani was too groggy to argue. "Did you get any sleep last night?"

"Some, but the rain kept me up. It didn't stop until a little while ago. I need to get home and check on my animals."

As plausible as that sounded, something felt off. Nick seemed tense.

Did he regret making love with her last night? Or even worse, had he somehow guessed that she loved him?

Swallowing back her anxiety, she managed a calm tone. "Are we okay, Nick?"

"Of course we are. We're still friends, and we always will be."

His smile reassured her that her secret was still safe, and that he had no clue that he owned her heart. Dani relaxed. "I'll text you this afternoon and let you know what time to meet me at the hospital," she reminded him.

"Great. I'll let myself out."

He dropped a quick kiss on the top of her head, the way he used to. Like a friend.

Then he was gone.

DETERMINED TO GET Dani and what they'd shared out of his head, Nick attacked the morning chores with a vengeance. As yet, the spring grass wasn't hearty enough to nourish the cattle, so he helped Blake and Wally load the flatbed with hay for them. It was hard work, and by the time the truck was loaded, he'd worked up quite a sweat. While they delivered the hay, he stayed in the barn.

The rain had stopped, but Nick's desire raged on. Even knowing he couldn't give Dani the love she deserved, he still wanted her. More than ever. Eager to forget his hunger, he approached his bay gelding, Benny. The horse's ears pricked forward in curiosity. "Morning," Nick said. "Hope you slept better than me. What do you say we take a ride?"

The animal neighed and Nick saddled him up. Moments later, they were trotting across the ranch. At some point, Nick sighted a calf, headed for a slippery ravine. Swearing softly, he dismounted, tethered Benny to a tree and on foot, chased the calf away from the precipice, slipping in the mud in the process.

Wet and filthy, he rode Benny back to the barn. After brushing down his horse, he stabled him. He changed clothes, then spent an hour or so tinkering with a tractor engine that kept stalling out. Inside the house again, he sat in the small room he used as an office and worked on creating a spreadsheet for next month's cattle market and paying bills.

And yet as busy as he was, for the first time ever, he couldn't shut off his thoughts or his feelings. If this had happened with any other woman Nick would have cut and run. He couldn't do that with Dani. He couldn't hurt her.

But he could put a stop to the physical side of their relationship. There would be no more incredible sex with her. He would explain tonight, after she had that talk with Big Mama.

He was eating lunch and damn it, fantasizing about Dani, when the rain began again, with a vengeance.

Lightning streaked across the sky, swiftly followed by ominous thunder. A loud *crack* shook the air.

Nick jumped up and raced through the back door, onto the porch. He didn't notice anything unusual, but he smelled smoke. It was coming from the south, in the direction of the barn.

The barn had been struck by lightning.

He pulled on his boots, shrugged into his jacket and headed outside. As he raced toward the barn, he slid his cell phone from his pocket and called Blake.

"That lightning you just heard hit the barn," he said as he ran. "Call the fire department, then get Wally and meet me there."

Both men arrived shortly after Nick. Smoke was pouring from the roof now, and they all heard the panicky squeals of the five terrified horses stabled inside.

Fearing the worst, Nick shouted out orders. "Blake, help me get these horses out of here. Wally, grab the fire extinguisher and do what you can."

Smoke filled the barn, and the air was hazy and thick with it. No wonder the horses were spooked. Leading them to safety wouldn't be easy.

Nick covered his mouth with a bandanna. Speaking in a low, calm voice, he approached Benny. "Easy, boy." The bay's eyes were wide with fear, but he allowed Nick to quickly bridle him and lead him out.

Blake led two other horses toward the door, the animals following Benny's lead. By the time all five were safely out of harm's way, the fire department had arrived.

Between putting out the fire, contacting the vet and meeting with the insurance adjustor, the hours flew by.

When Nick finally trudged toward the house, it was dark and he was tired, dirty, hungry and discouraged.

Nearly half the barn had been destroyed, the rest ruined by smoke damage. The new roof, only a month old, was too damaged to save, and the hay Nick had expected to last another week or so was ruined.

And just when he was getting closer to his goal.

The ranch insurance wouldn't cover much and he didn't have enough money to pay for this unexpected expense, meaning he'd have to borrow the rest. If, please God, all went well at the cattle market and his cattle fetched a decent price, he could pay off the debt and replenish his bank account. If not, he'd have to figure out another way to bring in some money.

Nick scrubbed a weary hand over his face. For every two steps the ranch progressed, it seemed to fall back one. He'd be damned if he'd fall into the same trap his father had, piling on the debt. Yet at times like this, he could understand why it had happened all those years ago. Unfortunately, his love for Nick's mother had only exacerbated the situation.

Nick tried to count his blessings. At least the fire had been contained quickly. It could have been a lot worse. When he got through this, and he would, he would open an account for emergencies, and make sure to add to it regularly.

He didn't check his cell phone until he'd showered and changed and grabbed something to eat. He noticed that Dani had texted him that she was on her way to the hospital and would see him soon. The message had been sent over an hour ago.

Nick swore. He'd promised to be there for her, and could only guess what she must be thinking. He wanted to call her, but by now she was probably talking to Big Mama. He sent a text instead.

Chapter Fourteen

Standing in the waiting room, Dani checked her cell phone for the dozenth time. She'd texted Nick over an hour ago to meet her at the hospital. When he hadn't replied, she'd left a voice message. She hadn't heard from him, nor had he shown up at the hospital.

Where was he? He knew how important this was, and how much she wanted him here today. She hoped everything was all right at the ranch. Deeper down, she wondered if the problem had to do with last night. This morning he'd assured her that things were fine between them. Maybe over the course of the day he'd changed his mind.

Dani didn't think she could bear that. But Nick wouldn't just pull away like that. Would he?

Her cell phone beeped, signaling a text message. It was from Nick. *Finally.* She blew out a relieved breath and read the screen.

Trouble at the ranch. Sorry I couldn't make it 2night. Call me when you're finished.

Her spirits sagged, and so did her courage. How was she going to do this without Nick?

You can do this, Dani. The mini pep talk she'd heard

from him too often to count popped into her mind and gave her the boost she needed. It was time for the dreaded heart-to-heart.

She hefted the get-well card from the restaurant and marched into her mother's room.

Wearing the robe Dani had brought her from home over her hospital gown, Big Mama was propped up in bed, reading a paperback. Her color was good. She looked like her normal self at bedtime, not an invalid recovering from surgery.

As soon as Dani entered, she set the book aside. "You're rarely late, but you are tonight. I was beginning to wonder. You must have been busy today."

"As if you didn't know. You only called four times to check on me."

"My, you're testy. I thought Nick was coming with you."

"He was supposed to meet me here, but something came up at the ranch."

"What's that you're carrying?"

"It's a card from our employees and customers."

Dani delivered it to her mother. The huge thing dwarfed her lap.

"Well, isn't this nice." Over her bifocals, she smiled at Dani. "Come over here, honey, while I read this."

Dani stood at her shoulder and read along with her.

Big Mama exclaimed over the messages. When she finished, she handed the card to Dani. "Put that on the windowsill so I can look at it." While Dani did that, her mother went on. "Thank them for me, will you?"

Dani nodded. Enough with the chit-chat. She pulled a chair to the side of the bed and squared her shoulders. "You and I need to talk."

"Should I be worried about the determined gleam in

your eyes?" Big Mama said. "Because if you're going to hound me about making changes to the restaurant, I've already said—"

"We'll discuss that later. This is about something else."

"Let me guess—you ran into some problems today at the restaurant that you didn't mention when I called." Big Mama shook her head. "I knew I should've talked Dr. Adelson and the nurses into letting me go home sooner so I could get back to work. What happened, Dani?"

Big Mama was really skilled at baiting her, but tonight Dani couldn't afford to let that bother her. "You haven't worked weekends for years, so you wouldn't have come in today, regardless. I handled any issues that came up as well as you would. And FYI, you're not going back to work until the doctor gives his okay, and even then only part-time." She spoke calmly and firmly.

"Part-time? No. I can't do that."

"You can, and you will." Big Mama's stubborn expression gave Dani pause, but at least she didn't argue.

"On the way home from the hospital Monday, we're stopping at the bank so that you can add me as co-owner on the business account," she went on. "You should probably also add me to your personal account. That way, if anything happens, I'll be able to pay the bills. I also want to set up a power of attorney, just in case."

Her mother looked taken aback. "You talk as if I'll be dead and buried tomorrow."

Dani agreed—that sounded extreme, and it made her feel terrible. She thought about dropping the subject and talking about something unemotional like the nasty weather, but she'd come too far to stop now.

Nick's words came back to her. *You can do this.*

After sucking in a fortifying breath, she went on. "I hope you live to be a hundred. But what I'm suggesting is the smart thing to do. You remember what happened when Nick's dad had his heart attack. No one could access his bank account, and it caused a lot of problems."

"I remember." Her mother sniffed, as if she was seriously put-out. "All right, I'll add you to both the accounts. But there's no need for you to be involved with either one right now. I'm perfectly capable of handling the money and bills myself."

Here goes. Dani cleared her throat. "According to the notice from the bank, you're not handling the restaurant's money so well."

Big Mama's jaw dropped in surprise. She could've won an acting award. "I have no idea what you're talking about."

"Don't play coy with me," Dani said. "I opened the mail yesterday. I read the overdraft notice."

Up went her mother's chin. "An overdraft isn't a crime."

"No, but it's expensive. Those bank fees add up, especially when you overdraw once or twice a month."

"You snooped through the bank statements?" Big Mama gave an indignant huff.

"That's right. Big Mama's Café is barely making it, and you didn't…" Dani stopped just short of accusing her mother of not trusting her. That wouldn't get her anywhere. "Why didn't you tell me?"

Uncharacteristically quiet, her mother fiddled with the sash of her robe.

"Is it…" Fear made Dani's throat go dry. Swallowing didn't work. She had to force the words out. "I don't understand why you don't trust me," she said, struggling to unclench her clasped hands.

"You're mumbling, Dani. What did you say?"

"I said—" Dani cleared her throat again. "I don't understand why you don't trust me. I'm your daughter."

There, the words were out. Hardly realizing what she was doing, she caught her breath and braced for the worst.

"Oh, honey, I do trust you." Her mother hung her head. Now she was the one speaking softly, and Dani barely made out the words. "I didn't say anything because I'm ashamed."

"Ashamed," Dani repeated. Of all the possible explanations she'd considered, she'd never imagined that her confident, independent mother would ever feel shame.

Big Mama gave a sheepish nod. "You've always looked up to me, and I've always stressed the importance of balancing your bank account. I couldn't bear for you to think less of me for my financial difficulties."

As proud as Big Mama was, Dani could only imagine how difficult it must be for her to admit this. "You're my mom," she said. "I'll always look up to you."

"Even when I make bad mistakes?"

"Who hasn't?"

"The restaurant would be all right if our business hadn't fallen off and I hadn't made some foolish investments a few years ago. Last year those investments went sour, and I haven't been able to catch up."

"I wish you'd just come out and told me right away." It would have saved Dani hours of anxiety and frustration. "Is that why you refuse to consider any of the changes to the restaurant that I've suggested?"

Her mother nodded. "We can't afford to make any."

"And yet if we don't, Big Mama's Café will never be what it used to be. Don't worry, we'll figure this out together. You really do trust me?" Dani asked, not quite believing it.

"Completely. I love you, honey."

Dani's relief was so great, she wanted to sob. "You, too."

"Are those tears I see?"

They were. Dani quickly swiped them away. "I'm just happy, Mom. Talking honestly with you feels good."

Nick had been right. Wait until he heard about this.

Something else occurred to her. "Is this why you're against hiring a health aide to take care of you when you get home? Because of the money?"

"I don't want anyone's help." Her mother compressed her lips. A moment later, she sighed. "But you're right, I also don't have the money to pay for an aide."

"Medicare will cover some of the cost," Dani said. "And I have enough money in my savings account to cover the rest."

"I can't ask you to use your hard-earned savings on me, Dani. That's for a rainy day."

"This *is* my rainy day," she said. "I'm your daughter, and I want to help." She'd use any money left over to upgrade the restaurant. "I'll make some calls right away and line up someone before Monday."

"I see by the look on your face that you won't take 'no' for an answer." Big Mama shook her head. "Why am I not surprised? All right, go ahead, but I will pay you back. Make sure you get a woman—I don't want a man prowling around the house."

"Okay. If we're lucky, she'll be able to come over Monday to meet you. And the best way to repay me? Trust me to manage the restaurant."

"I do, but—"

Dani held up her hand, palm up, until her mother closed her mouth. "If you *really* trust me, here's how to prove it." She used her fingers, ticking off each item on her list. "First, no more calling me during work hours unless it's a medical emergency. Second, we share the bill-paying responsibilities for the restaurant. And third, if I come up with low-cost ways to modernize the restaurant, I get a chance to test them. Do we have a deal?"

"Do I have a choice?" her mother countered.

Dani shook her head.

"Then, I guess we have a deal."

Dani's fears and worries slipped away, and suddenly she felt worlds lighter, as well as empowered and heard. "Excellent."

"I guess I should thank you for talking to me about these things, Dani."

"This conversation was long overdue. Next time you have a problem, share it with me."

"As long as you do the same. Now come give your Big Mama a hug. Then go home, and let me get some sleep."

Dani was smiling as she left her mother's room. She wished Nick had been with her tonight. He'd be so proud of her.

He was waiting to hear from her, and she was eager to talk to him. She was also curious about what had happened at the ranch. It must have been pretty bad to keep him away.

As soon as she slid into the driver's seat of her car, she speed-dialed him.

NICK WAS SPRAWLED in the recliner, mindlessly stuffing popcorn into his mouth, channel-surfing and wondering about Dani and her mom, when she called at last.

"Hey, Dani." He turned off the tube.

"I was so worried earlier," she said. "Are you okay? What happened at the ranch?"

"We had an emergency this afternoon and I lost track of the time. That's why I texted you back so late, and why

I couldn't make it to the hospital." He felt bad about that. "You were counting on me to be there when you talked to your mom, and I'm awful sorry I wasn't there. How did it go?"

"First I want to hear what happened at the ranch. You said there was trouble?"

"I'll explain in a minute. Tell me about Big Mama."

"I did it, Nick—I talked to her." She sounded pleased with herself. "And it went better than I expected."

For the first time in hours, he smiled. "Yeah?"

"Uh-huh. You'll never guess why she never mentioned those overdrafts. She was ashamed. She thought I'd think less of her."

"Seriously? You're right, I would never have guessed."

"Me, either. I took your advice and reminded her what a mess you and your family were stuck with when your father died and you couldn't get into his account. She agreed to add me as a co-owner of both the business and personal accounts. We're going to stop at the bank on the way home from the hospital."

"Wow. I'm impressed."

"I can hardly believe it myself. Oh, I also laid down the law. She agreed not to call me on her days off unless it's a medical emergency. We're going to share the bill-paying responsibilities, *and* she's going to let me make some changes to the restaurant. Is that cool, or what?"

Dani sounded so happy, that Nick's own spirits lifted. "I'd say you hit the jackpot tonight. I'm proud of you, Dani."

"Thanks. I'm sorry you missed all the fun. So what happened to you?"

He'd have preferred to forget about that for a little while, but he wanted to tell her. "You know how bad the lightning has been. This afternoon, one 'lucky' strike hit the barn."

She made a horrified sound. "Oh, no, Nick. Please tell me that your crew and the horses are okay."

"When it happened, only Wally, Blake and I were here. Palmer, Clip and Jerome didn't come back until later. We got the horses safely out. They were pretty spooked, and they inhaled some smoke, but the vet examined them and said they seemed all right."

Dani let out a loud breath. "That's a relief."

"Don't I know it. Still, to be on the safe side, Clip's going to bunk with the horses tonight and keep an eye on them."

"Not in the barn, though, huh?"

"In one of the sheds." An old but solid structure that had housed supplies and various spare machine parts. "The crew put up five makeshift stalls. The horses settled right in."

"How damaged is the barn?" Dani asked.

Just thinking about that made Nick feel weary clear to his bones. He closed his eyes and massaged the place between his eyebrows. "It's bad. The fire department did their best, but what the fire didn't destroy, smoke damage did. The whole thing is pretty much totaled. We were able to salvage the saddles and horse tackle, but the feed and hay are gone."

"Oh, no," Dani said. "I'm so sorry. And after all the time, work and money you put into building the new roof."

"It's a bummer, all right." Absently Nick rubbed his shoulder, which he'd somehow strained during all the chaos. "The foundation is fine, but I'm going to have to rebuild the rest."

"Not by yourself, I hope. I remember what happened

when you tried to make a doghouse in high school shop class."

"You remember that lopsided disaster?" Nick chuckled at the memory, and was surprised that she'd managed to coax a laugh out of him. "I'll help with the barn, but a contractor I know is coming out tomorrow to give me an estimate."

"Good luck. Hey, it's early yet, and after my talk with Big Mama, I'm too keyed up to sleep. I could come over tonight," Dani said, sounding slightly breathless at the idea. "I'll bring something to help you feel better. What would you like—cookies? Ice cream? Me? Or all three."

Nick seriously considered the tempting offer. But she was in love with him, and for that reason, he had to keep his distance.

"Neither of us slept much last night, and I'm dead on my feet," he said. That was true. "Plus, we both have to get up at the crack of dawn and work tomorrow."

"As usual, you're right. Sleep well, Nick."

"I will. You, too."

"No 'sweet dreams, Dani?'" she asked.

"Sweet dreams, Dani," he echoed, hoping her dreams weren't about him.

Chapter Fifteen

"Denise seems wonderful," Dani commented after the home health aide left Big Mama's house on Monday afternoon. They'd barely gotten home from the bank when the woman had arrived. In her fifties and seemingly friendly and competent, she'd stayed about an hour, asking questions and jotting down notes while she talked with Dani and Big Mama.

Even better, she was available to start tomorrow morning. She wasn't going to stay all day—Big Mama didn't need that kind of care—but knowing somone would be with her lifted a huge burden off Dani's shoulders.

"She claims she can make the blandest diet taste great," Dani went on. "It'll be nice to have her cook your meals, bring in the mail, clean house and drive you to your doctor's appointments."

"I suppose," Big Mama grumbled.

"I thought you liked her."

"What does that have to do with anything? I like most people." Her mother all but rolled her eyes. "But I hate not being able to drive or care for myself."

"It's only for a few weeks. Besides, it's not as if you're an invalid. You can shower, feed and dress yourself. You can also take walks. And just imagine all the books you'll finally have a chance to read. Maybe you'll even watch a few episodes of *Restaurant: Impossible.* That might help you get some low-cost ideas for the restaurant."

"Those things will hardly fill up the day. I don't know how I'm supposed to sit around here when I'm used to working. I'd rather be at the restaurant to put out fires and keep it running smoothly."

"Uh-uh-uh." Dani waggled her finger at her mother. "You're going to trust me to do those things, remember?"

"I remember." Suddenly looking very tired, Big Mama yawned.

"It's been a really busy day," Dani said. "Why don't you lie down for a while, and I'll run out and pick up groceries for the week. What should we have for dinner?"

"You're staying for dinner?"

Not about to leave her mother alone on her first night home, Dani nodded. "I'll leave when you're in bed tonight and ready to go to sleep."

"Just cook something you want."

"All right, I'll pick up some fish to broil." Broiled fish wasn't at the top of Dani's favorite foods list, but it was supposed to be good for her mother's heart.

Her mother wrinkled her nose. "Couldn't you fry it instead?"

"You're not supposed to have fried foods."

"Does Nick know that I've been discharged from the hospital?"

Dani nodded.

Big Mama brightened. "Let's invite him over for dinner, to celebrate that I'm home and on the mend. After working on that barn mess and all the other ranch responsibilities the poor man is dealing with, he's bound to appreciate the invitation for a home-cooked meal. The three of us at my dinner table—it'll be like the old days."

Not the same at all. A great deal had happened since

those days. Dani and Nick had made love. Now he owned her heart. The challenge was to keep him from finding out.

"And you can cook something he likes—meatloaf or pot roast," Big Mama added. "Neither are fried."

Laughing, Dani shook her head. "You're incorrigible. You know you're supposed to cut way down on red meat. Tonight, we're eating broiled fish. But inviting Nick is a great idea. I'll give him a call."

"Do that," her mother said. "Now I'm going to lie down."

Dani headed for her car. On this last day of March, the sky was a brilliant blue and the air was warm enough for only a sweater. Enjoying the sun on her face, she sat down on the bottom porch step and dialed Nick.

"Hi," she said.

"Hey. Hold on a sec." He covered the phone, but she heard him say, "It's Dani. I'll be just a minute."

"I hear pounding in the background," she said.

"The contractor will be here first thing tomorrow, and Blake, Wally and I are busting up the last of the barn to get ready for him. We're tossing what we can't reuse into a flatbed. They'll haul it to the burn pile."

"Sounds as if you're making progress. We have, too. We met Big Mama's home health aide. She's great, and she also starts tomorrow. Big Mama's at home now, and ta-da—I'm officially the co-owner of both the business checking and her personal accounts."

"Way to go. I'll bet she's *real* happy to have someone come in and fuss over her."

Dani smiled at his teasing tone. "She's complaining about it, all right. But as I reminded her, it's only for a few weeks. Right now, she's taking a nap and I'm about to pick up some groceries for the week. We'd love for you to join us for dinner tonight."

Nick hesitated just long enough for Dani to wonder why.

"I would, but there's so much to do around here," he said. "You should see the mess. It has to be cleaned up today."

"We aren't planning to eat until after sunset. Surely you won't be working in the dark."

"There's too much to do," he repeated. "I can't make it."

Now she felt downright uncomfortable. "I know you have a lot on your plate," she said. "But something's weird."

"How so?"

Dani had to mull that over for a moment. "You're… You seem distant. Is it because we made love the other night?"

Nick's second, longer hesitation all but gave her the answer to her question and filled her with dread.

"This isn't a conversation I want to have right now," he said.

Ominous words. Her heart stuttered in her chest.

She was such a dunce. Nick couldn't have realized she loved him or he would have done more than pull away, but he was still wary. So what was his problem?

Dani gave her forehead a mental smack. "I'm not like the other women you've slept with, Nick. I'm not chasing after you."

"Did I say I thought you were?"

"I know how your mind works. FYI, inviting you to dinner tonight was Big Mama's idea, not mine. It's just a meal."

"I get that."

"Could've fooled me." She was getting angry. "What's the deal, Nick?"

"Come on, Dani. Now isn't the time or the place."

He wanted her to drop it, but something inside her wouldn't let her. "The time or place for what? I have no idea what you're talking about. But then, that's your M.O."

"What the hell does that mean?"

"It means that whenever you're involved with a woman and things start to get too deep, you walk away and never look back. Not that this is remotely like a breakup. It can't be—I'm not your girlfriend."

She almost choked on her words. Because this definitely *was* a breakup. Her heart ached as if it had been ripped into pieces. "I can guess what comes next—you're going to say that you need your space."

He didn't refute her words. "Maybe we should talk about this in person," he said.

Let him see her cry over him? Never. "You know what? Forget about dinner. I could use some space, too, so if you have anything else to say, you'd best say it now."

"Dani," he said, sounding sad and weary. "I don't want to hurt you."

"Too late. Goodbye, Nick." She disconnected.

Next door, Gumbo woofed and trotted to the chain-link fence for a pat. "Not now," she said as the tears began to flow.

Sitting in the car with the windows rolled up, shaking and bawling, she wanted to drive straight to Lannigan's for a gallon of rocky road, then go home and distract herself with a three-hanky movie.

But her mother needed her. There was nothing to do but hold herself together.

Dani blew her nose, sat up straighter and reminded

herself that at least Nick hadn't figured out she loved him. That was something to be grateful for.

As she headed for the grocery, she found an oldies station on the radio. "Garden Party," the Rick Nelson oldie, was playing. *"You can't please everyone, so you've got to please yourself."*

Dani was too downcast to sing along, but as she listened to the words, a new resolve hatched in her chest. She agreed wholeheartedly with Rick Nelson.

She was through trying to please other people. Specifically men. Ironic that Nick had been encouraging her to do just that for ages, and that during their love-making, he'd shown her the joys of putting her own pleasure first.

From now on she was going to do just that—please herself.

FRIDAY EVENING, DANI sat at Big Mama's kitchen table, picking at her meal. Her mother seemed to be feeling better. Just tonight, she'd become more talkative and less irritable. While Dani was the opposite.

"Denise's cooking is growing on me," Big Mama commented. "This low-fat casserole is surprisingly tasty."

She said something else, but Dani tuned her out. It had been four days, but she hadn't told her mother or anyone else about Nick yet. The end of their friendship was too new and she was still too raw.

"Dani!"

Dani jerked to attention. "Did you want something?"

"I said, I don't think you care for this casserole."

She'd sampled a few bites, but in her opinion, the stuff was tasteless. But lately, everything tasted blah. "It's not bad," she said.

Her mother eyed her. "I'm recuperating from surgery,

but you seem to be the one who's sick. I know you've been working extra hard at the restaurant, but still. You haven't been acting like your usual self for days now. I hope you're not coming down with something."

"If I were, I wouldn't be here. I'd never expose you to anything."

"Well, you certainly are worried about something. You don't have to protect me. I'm not that frail. Is the bank account overdrawn again?"

Dani shook her head. "Everything's fine at the restaurant."

Now that she had her mother's okay to make some changes at Big Mama's Café, she'd begun to look seriously at low-cost options, searching for sales and high-quality discount stores. Finally having the freedom to do what she knew in her bones was the right thing for the restaurant was exciting. At least it should have been. As downhearted as she was right now, it wasn't easy to muster up much enthusiasm.

"I'm trying to be cheerful so that I'll heal faster, but your mood is depressing me." Her mother gave her the pointed, no-nonsense look that meant she expected an explanation.

Should she share her troubles or not? Dani tried to gauge whether she was strong enough to tell her mother about Nick without breaking down. For the past four nights, she'd cried herself to sleep, often feeling as if she'd never stop. She didn't want to get that emotional now.

Her debate lasted all of a few seconds before she came to a decision. She *needed* to talk about this. Why not with her mother? For that matter, why not tell Lana, and Christy, Becca, Janelle and everyone else? Sooner or later they were all bound to find out. The story may as well come from her own lips.

"You're right, I am in bad mood," she said. "Nick and I…" Getting the words out wasn't easy. A huge lump formed in her throat, and tears gathered behind her eyes. "We broke up."

Her mother seemed puzzled. "How can you break up when you've never been boyfriend and girlfriend?"

"That's a very good question." Dani smoothed her napkin over her lap and pulled herself together. "The thing is, my feelings for Nick have moved beyond friendship. Unfortunately, his for me haven't," she summarized. Right now, that was the best she could manage.

"But you're perfect for each other. I've always said so."

"Please don't, Mom."

"Oh, honey. That must hurt."

"It does." Big Mama had no idea, and her sympathetic expression only made things worse. Dani bit her lip against a rush of pain and heartache. "We decided not to see each other anymore."

"Not ever?"

They hadn't discussed how much space they both needed, but Dani knew the answer. This time, the tears behind her eyes leaked out. "Never."

Big Mama's eyes filled, too. "Whose decision was that?" she asked, sniffling.

Dani doubted she could handle a cry-fest with her mother. Making a monumental effort, she sucked in a calming breath and brushed her tears away. "It was mutual."

"But he's been in your life for so many years. Are you sure this is what you want?"

Dani couldn't lie. "No, it isn't."

"What's the matter with Nick, agreeing to something like that? I'm going to call that boy and give him a piece of my mind."

"Please don't. He's always been honest with me. It's not his fault I fell in love with him." Her own reasonable tone amazed her. She sounded calm and rational, when inside she was a tangled up mass of pain.

By her mother's widened eyes, she was similarly surprised. "You're not upset with Nick?"

Dani shook her head. "At the moment life seems pretty awful, but eventually I'll be okay."

"Of course you will. Still, I hate that you're hurting."

"I've been hurt before, and I always manage to bounce back. I'm a survivor."

Her mother gave her a watery smile. "That you are, from the time you were a little scrapper and I first took you in. Some kids take days or weeks to adjust, but you? It was obvious that you were scared, but you were so brave. You came in and made yourself at home. Then and there, I decided that I wanted you for my own daughter."

For some reason, the words bolstered Dani's morale. "Do you remember about a month ago, when you and I had cinnamon rolls together, right here at this table?" she asked. It seemed eons ago. Dani waited for her mother's nod. "You said then that I don't need a man to be happy. At the time, I blew it off, but lately I've been thinking a lot about it. Now don't go into shock, but I've decided you're right."

Her mother pantomimed exactly that, widening her eyes and dropping her jaw. Dani almost smiled.

"I can definitely be happy without a man," she said. "From now on, I'm going to put myself first and do what pleases me. You'll see."

Her mother absorbed this in silence before she spoke again. "That sounds very wise, Dani. And I'm certain that Nick will come to his senses. He's going to miss you and your friendship terribly."

"I'm not so sure that he will." Dani was tired of talking about her broken heart. "Can we change the subject now? I want to run something by you. It's about the restaurant."

"So you have more ideas about the changes you're going to make. I can't wait to hear them."

Her mother's one-eighty attitude adjustment was amazing, but since Dani had agreed to stick to a low-cost budget, paid for with funds from her own savings, her mother had actually grown excited about the restaurant facelift. That was something to be grateful for. Though with Dani also paying part of the cost of the home health aide, she didn't have as much money to spend as she would have liked. By necessity, she'd pared down the renovations she wanted to make.

"This isn't about a change, exactly, but it is related," Dani said. "I keep remembering how everyone signed that get-well card for you. They care about both you and the restaurant, and I'm sure they want it to be here for many years to come. Why not announce that we're going to make updates to boost business, and ask them for their ideas?"

Her mother sniffed. "Airing our private problems with customers or anyone else doesn't sit well with me. Neither does asking for help."

Dani understood and normally she would have agreed. But she was into pleasing herself now, and ensuring a long, profitable future for Big Mama's Café definitely pleased her. Wasn't that more important than hiding the restaurant's problems and letting the business slide even further into the red?

"When I had that trouble with Charlie and then when you were in the hospital, I learned just how much our customers and employees care about us," she said. "I say we swallow our pride, admit that we're in trouble and see where it takes us."

"I vote no, but it's your savings account and your future. Besides, it's obvious from the expression on your face that you've already made up your mind."

This was her mother's way of showing that she trusted Dani to do what was right for them both and for Big Mama's Café. Dani was happy about that. At least this part of her life was on track. It helped to salve the gaping hole in her heart.

THE FOLLOWING MORNING, Dani arrived at Big Mama's Café with the hand-lettered poster she'd made the night before. It had taken a while for her to come up with just the right wording, but focusing on the sign had beat moping around, crying over Nick.

Before propping the poster on an easel beside the hostess desk, she turned it around backward and set it aside. Last night she'd asked the entire Saturday staff—Naomi, the forty-four year old weekend hostess, Sadie, Colleen, Mike, Jeff—who also cooked—and the busboys, Carl and Gene, to come in thirty minutes early, for a meeting. She'd also invited Shelby and Melanie. It was still dark out, and everyone yawned sleepily, but Sadie had made coffee.

"You're all aware that business has been steadily falling off for a while now," Dani said after they filled their mugs. "We're in trouble."

The staff exchanged worried looks.

"Are we going to lose our jobs?" Sadie asked, clutching her hands together at the waist. She was suddenly wide-awake.

"Not if we make some changes that bring in new customers. This restaurant needs a facelift and a revised menu, and for that, we're going to require help."

"What kind of help?" Mike asked. "Are you talking about money?"

Admitting she needed help was one thing, but soliciting money? At the very idea, Dani's stomach balled into a knot of unease. "We are on a strict budget, but I'm leaning more toward finding experts who are willing to work for a discount," she said. "Some of our regulars are carpenters and electricians. I'm hoping to work a trade of sorts—free meals in exchange for a lower fee."

"That's a great idea," Shelby said. "But I don't know why we shouldn't ask for money, too."

"We could host a fund-raiser!" Colleen brightened up. "We did that at Serena's—" her daughter's "—school. People who donated wrote their names on slips of paper and put them in a box. At the end of the fund-raiser we drew some of the names for prizes. It was a big success."

"What kinds of prizes?" Sadie asked. "Dani probably doesn't have much money for that."

Mike stroked his chin. "How about a free breakfast or lunch, or we could name a new dish after the person whose slip we draw." He glanced at Dani.

She barely had a chance to mull that over before Colleen added her two cents.

"We could have two containers—one for the donations, and the other for the names of each donor. We'll draw several and offer the winners the choice of the free meal or having a dish named after them."

The whole staff was getting excited now, and so was Dani. The idea of giving out prizes in exchange for donations wasn't half bad, and the knots in her stomach loosened. "I'll consider it," she said.

As if she hadn't commented, they went right on planning.

"I just tossed an empty coffee can into the kitchen trash," Mike said. "I'll pull it out."

"I'll cut a slit for the money in the plastic lid," Jeff volunteered.

"I'll wash it," Carl offered.

Colleen nodded enthusiastically. "I just emptied a box of sugar packets. We can use it for names. I also happen to have a bag full of art scraps in the car, left over from an art project at Serena's school. I'll pick something from there to decorate the box and the can."

Sadie smiled. "I'll cut strips of paper for people who donate to write their names on."

"Can employees donate?" Gene asked. "I'll put in five bucks."

"Me, too," Melanie said.

"I'll make flyers and bring them in on Monday," Shelby offered.

"We can tack them up all over town," Mike said.

They were all so gung-ho that Dani decided to swallow her pride whole hog. "All right," she said. "Let's do it."

Sadie nodded at the poster. "Show us the sign."

Dani propped it on the easel.

Help us save Big Mama's Café! Ask us what you can do.

The waitress clapped her hands. "It's perfect!"

"Thanks, Sadie. Thank you all." Dani smiled and checked her watch. "We open in less than thirty minutes. Let's get busy."

By the end of the day, she'd lined up a printer who'd agreed to do the new menus in exchange for a few months' worth of free brunches. An interior designer who was new in the business had offered to provide free consulting services, just to get the experience. And the restaurant had collected almost a hundred dollars.

Not bad for one day. Dani had to pinch herself to make sure it was real. She high-fived her staff and let out several hi-pitched *squees*. They were off to a great start.

Chapter Sixteen

On a late Friday afternoon in mid-April, Nick stood in line at Carson Building Supply to pay for some building supplies for the barn.

"How's that new barn coming along?" asked Marty Sloan, a short, round clerk who'd been handling the cash register since Nick had first come into the store as a kid with his dad. Marty was a big gossip, and over the years Nick had learned to choose his words with care.

"Not bad," he said. "If all goes well, I'll able to stable the horses in there next week, a few days ahead of schedule."

As great news as that was, Nick couldn't summon up much enthusiasm. Nearly a month after his split with Dani, he was still messed up, and his dark mood colored everything—his work, his sleep—his *life*.

Which was pretty damn ironic, considering that their "breakup" was supposed to have kept his focus on the ranch instead of her.

She'd given him what he wanted—plenty of space. They knew a lot of the same people and frequented many of the same places, but both to his relief and his disappointment, he hadn't seen or spoken with her since the day she'd called to invite him to her mom's for dinner. The day their relationship had imploded.

He was still kicking himself for the way that had gone down. A couple of times over the past few weeks, he'd reached for the phone, just to hear her voice and check on her. He'd always stopped himself. Contacting her would only make things worse.

"Going to the cattle market next weekend?" Marty asked.

"Wouldn't miss it." Thanks to a diet of lush spring grass, Nick's livestock had gained weight steadily, which would help him get a good price for them.

"Ranchers come away from that market flush with cash," Marty said. "Sure is great for our business."

Tired of making small talk, Nick frowned. "I should get going. Is there a problem?"

Marty banged on his cash register. "Darned computer's awful slow today. It'll come back up in a minute. You look tired, Nick, even for this time of year. Putting in extra long hours?"

"Yep."

Yet as long and hard as Nick worked each day—and most days he pushed himself until he was ready to keel over, trying to banish Dani from his thoughts—she was always with him. Even in his dreams.

Penance for screwing things up with her, for doing the one thing he'd sworn never to do. Hurting her.

Which made him the number one ass of the year.

He'd heard that she was getting ready to make some of the changes at Big Mama's Café that she'd talked about. Apparently she'd held some kind of fund-raiser, which surprised him. She wasn't one to ask for that kind of help. Wanting to donate, but not about to set foot in the restaurant, he'd made an anonymous cash donation through the mail. It didn't make up for what he'd done—nothing could—but at least it was something.

Marty gave him a shrewd look. "It's all over town that you and Dani broke up. Funny, huh, when you two have never been together."

Forgetting to watch himself around the clerk, Nick scowled. "Who the hell told you that?"

"It's just something I heard. I see from your reaction that you and Dani *were* involved." The computer beeped, and Marty tapped a few keys on the keyboard. "Ah, we're up again. All these years, I assumed you two were just friends."

Nick narrowed his eyes. "How much do I owe you, Marty?"

The clerk hastily totaled the amount. "As always, your order will be waiting for you at the delivery dock."

Moments later, Nick slid into the truck. He drove it to the pickup area and loaded the supplies.

On the drive to the ranch he found a jazz station and cranked up the radio, hoping the beat and the loud music would silence his mind.

No such luck. He missed Dani more than he'd ever imagined.

But even if he did feel like crap, steering clear of her was for the best, he assured himself. She needed time to get over him.

Then maybe he could fill the hole in his chest and he could start enjoying his life again.

SEWING MACHINES AND fabric littered Janelle's dining room table. Dani glanced approvingly at the stack of curtains she, Janelle, Becca and Christy had sewn in just a few hours.

"I never could have made all these myself," she said. "What a lucky break that you were all free and willing to give up your Saturday afternoon for this."

Since she'd broken off with Nick almost a month ago, her friends had spent a fair amount of time with her.

The past few weeks had been especially busy. Asking for help had yielded results Dani could never have imagined. The restaurant regulars were almost as vested as she was in turning business around at Big Mama's Café, and had jumped at the idea of helping.

Boy, had they. The fund-raising can had quickly filled—numerous times. She'd even received an anonymous cash donation. Combined with the money from her savings and the discounts from the carpenter and electrician—who'd agreed to lower their rates in exchange for free meals—there was enough to do almost everything Dani envisioned.

Awarding free meals and naming menu items after donors seemed small prices to pay for revitalizing Big Mama's Café.

After weeks of hard work, everything was coming together. Exactly one week from tomorrow, Big Mama's Café would close so that Dani's dreams for the restaurant could at last become a reality. She could hardly wait.

She smiled at her friends. "Have I told you lately that you're the best?"

"Only a couple times." Christy laughed.

"I'm glad I could make it today," Becca said. "Sewing with you guys has been fun—almost as much fun as that silk painting class we took. If you leave out Christy's meltdown that day."

"Come on, ladies," Christy said. "Everyone suffers pre-wedding jitters."

She and Per had compromised over the wedding. It was still going to be held at the Falls, but had been scaled down to a less costly event.

"Pre-pre-pre wedding jitters," Janelle teased. "I don't

care that much about sewing, but I'll do anything for chocolate." She helped herself to the last chocolate melt-away in the hefty bag of goodies Dani had brought over. "Chocolate *and* dinner on Dani tonight? Who needs a date when I've got my three amigos to party with?"

"And just think, we're contributing to the new and improved Big Mama's Café." Becca blew on her nails and polished them on her blouse. "The restaurant is going to look so cool with our curtains hanging in the windows. This is such great fabric. The artsy cartoon sketches of people eating makes me smile, and the colors are so bright and fun."

Dani agreed. "Which is exactly the mood I'm going for. Would you believe I got it on sale?"

"Who knew you were such a talented bargain shopper?" Christy said. "I should hire you to help with my wedding."

As pleased as Dani was for her friend, all that joy was painful to witness. She shook her head. "No way. I already have my hands full with the restaurant."

Between running the business, streamlining her plans and visiting and consulting with Big Mama, she barely had a moment to think. Which was good. It saved her from continually dissolving into tears.

She'd assured Big Mama that she could be happy without a man, and she was determined to prove it to herself. She wasn't there by a long shot, but she was confident that eventually she would be.

"I can't believe that in just seven days, you'll be closing Big Mama's doors for a whole week," Becca lamented. "Where will I go for Sunday brunch?"

"We won't be closed any Sunday, not even next week—if you come before noon," Dani said. "That's when we're locking the doors so that we can start the remodel. Monday doesn't count, because we're always closed Mondays. So really, we're only closed four days, Tuesday through Friday. Two weeks from today, on Saturday, we re-open."

Dani and everyone she'd hired would need every second of that time to complete the remodel.

"How about a sneak peek?" Christy said. "Do you have any sketches to show us? Or if you don't have those with you, at least give us an idea of what Big Mama's will look like."

Dani shook her head. "No way—it's a surprise. Come to the grand reopening and you'll find out."

"But we're your BFFs," Janelle pushed. "You have to give us preferential treatment."

They were supportive and wonderful friends, and Dani loved them dearly. But she doubted she'd ever feel as close to them as she had to Nick. Theirs had been a rare friendship that could never be duplicated.

"No can do." She smiled. "But I will tell you that Sly will be installing some amazing new light fixtures."

"Sly on a ladder—there's a sight I'd pay to see. Lana's so lucky." Janelle let out an admiring sigh. "Speaking of your brother, does he still want to deck Nick?"

"Probably, but I've warned him that I'll kill him if he tries."

Like everyone else, Sly knew that her friendship with Nick had crashed and burned. His protective, big-brother gene had kicked in, but Dani had stated in no uncertain terms that what had happened was none of Sly's business—or anyone else's, for that matter—and had ordered him to mind his own business.

"What about Big Mama?" Christy asked. "Is she still upset about Nick?"

Her mother had been reasonably understanding, but she also continued to bug Dani to make up with him.

She hadn't heard from him in weeks, which told her everything she needed to know about that. There wasn't going to be any making up.

"The past few days, she finally stopped bringing up his name," she said. "Now, with so much about to happen at the restaurant, she's been distracted—thank You, God."

"So your mom's cool with closing the restaurant for a few days?" Christy asked.

"She's pretty excited. She can hardly wait for the grand reopening."

"Will she be well enough to attend?" Janelle asked.

Dani nodded. "It's been almost six weeks since the surgery. She's just about back to normal, and her cardiologist has already given her the okay—as long as she promises not to stay too long. He says that if all goes well, she'll be able to return to work soon. But only for a few hours a day, a couple days a week."

Becca snorted. "As if she'll settle for that."

"She will, or I'll send her straight home," Dani said.

"Listen to you, all take-charge." Janelle shook her head. "Things have really turned around between you. I never imagined you'd get there."

"Your new 'please myself' plan is really working for you, Dani." Christy gave a thumbs-up.

Dani agreed. "I wish I'd figured it out ages ago." If she had, she'd probably have saved herself a lot of headaches and heartache—especially the biggest heartache.

As things stood, she was definitely not going to attend Nick's mother's wedding. Instead of contacting Nick, she'd phoned his mother directly. The woman hadn't heard that their friendship had ended, and had been shocked.

As was Dani—still. Even now, accepting what had happened was difficult. Nick had been her best friend for over half her life, and she missed him terribly. It was as if a part of her had died. She was trying hard not to think about him, a Herculean task that was all but impossible.

And certainly leeched the joy out of the rest of her life.

Not that she wasn't grateful for everything that was happening at the restaurant. It was just that sometimes she felt as if she would never be happy again.

She was ready to give up on the dream of finding her Mr. Right. In a way, she'd become a lot like Nick. A twist he'd probably appreciate. Only he would never know.

Here she was, all sad again, and her friends were openly scrutinizing her. If they guessed how miserable she still felt, the entire evening would become a giant "poor Dani" party. She smiled brightly. "Help me lay these curtains in the trunk of my car, and then let's go eat!"

They gave her sympathetic looks. So much for fooling them.

"Are you sure you're up to going out tonight?" Christy asked.

"Definitely. Lately Big Mama and the restaurant have taken up all my waking hours. Tonight, I could use some fun."

"All right, then." Becca squared her shoulders, the picture of a determined woman. "Where do you want to go?"

"Someplace with tasty food and a live band. How about the—"

"Bitter & Sweet!" Becca, Janelle and Christy chimed in unison.

Everyone laughed, Dani included.

"It's been a while since I danced," she said. Since before she and Jeter had broken up. A lifetime ago.

"Let's take separate cars," Christy said. "That way when I'm ready to go home to my sweetie, you three can stay out and keep partying…"

"Great idea," Dani said. "We'll meet there."

The Bitter & Sweet was packed, as it always was on a Saturday night. Despite the palpable energy in the room, the fabulous food and frequent bouts of laughter, Dani was drained by the time she finished her dessert and was ready to leave. A few minutes before the band was due to come on stage, she signaled for the check.

"I changed my mind about dancing," she told her friends in her new please-myself mode. "You know how busy the restaurant is on Sunday mornings. Plus, I still have a lot to do before the remodel. I'm going home."

It was obvious that they were disappointed. The old Dani would have put on a happy face and stayed to please them. The new Dani was unapologetic. "Quit worrying about me and enjoy yourselves," she told them. "I'll see you all in a couple of weeks, at the grand reopening of Big Mama's Café."

Chapter Seventeen

"Happy, boss?" Palmer asked as he and Nick sat in a tavern after the close of the Saturday cattle market.

Nick's livestock had sold for record prices. Once again, he was in the black—and then some. A big relief. He'd pay off his loan and padded the account he'd earmarked for emergencies.

He patted the fat check in his pocket. "I'm doin' okay."

"It's been a decent year, not counting what happened to the barn. And even that turned out okay in the end. The new one will last for decades." Resting his forearms on the table, Palmer shook his head. "I've watched this ranch almost fail under the people who owned it before you, but now that you're in charge... You're focused, you have smarts and plenty of can-do attitude. That's a potent combination, and I have a strong hunch you'll make this ranch fly."

High praise from the seasoned foreman. Nick dipped his head. "Appreciate that."

"Let's toast Kelly Ranch and your good fortune." Palmer raised his mug.

When Nick joined in half-heartedly, Palmer studied him. "I thought for sure that big check would ease the load off your shoulders. But you're as down as a newborn calf without its mother. You've been in a crappy mood for weeks, and I'm sick of it. I'm not the only, either."

In no mood for a lecture, Nick narrowed his eyes. "Save the pep talk for someone who needs it."

"That would be you. If you miss Dani, talk to her."

It seemed everyone had heard about him and Dani. The looks and whispers only made it harder to forget what had happened. "You can go to hell," Nick growled, setting his mug down none too gently. "I'm outta here."

His foreman muttered something about the stick up Nick's butt as he followed Nick to the truck, but after that he kept his big mouth shut. Smart man, Palmer.

Traffic was light. The sun had dropped low in the sky, and vivid pink streaks accented the horizon. It was the kind of evening Dani would say was made for romance.

In a worse mood than ever, Nick scowled at nothing at all.

They weren't far from the ranch when his damned foreman started up again. "Next Saturday, Big Mama's Café is having their grand reopening. I'm taking Pam over there for breakfast. You going?"

"Probably not," Nick said. "My mom's getting married next weekend."

Palmer made an *are you kidding me?* face. "She's getting married on Friday. Look, I realize you and Dani aren't getting along, but she'll have your hide if you're not there."

"She doesn't want to see me."

Nick missed her more every day. His chest felt like there was a gaping hole in it. Everything seemed colorless and dull, even the brilliant sunset.

"How can you be so sure she doesn't want to see you?" Palmer asked.

Because it would take her a while to get over him. Nick shrugged. "I just do."

"You two have always been like *this*." Palmer pressed two fingers together and held them up. "In the two years that I've known you both, you've never had anything close to a fight. You must've done something really bad."

Wasn't that the truth. Nick had hurt her, and in the process he'd also hurt himself. Forgetting he'd yelled at Palmer to back off moments ago, he blew out a heavy breath. "I really screwed up."

"What exactly did you do?"

He glanced away from the road to glare at his foreman. "Don't push it, Palmer."

Unperturbed, the foreman calmly met his gaze. "Whatever you did, fix it. Or I swear, I'll smack you upside the head."

"You would, too," Nick grumbled. "Maybe I can't fix it."

"Have you tried?"

Nick debated how to reply. "Dani needs space," he summarized. "So do I."

Palmer snorted. "Yeah, I can see that."

When Nick let loose with a string of oaths, the foreman shook his head. "From time to time every man needs his space, but come on, enough is enough. I doubt Dani's any happier about whatever's keeping you apart than you are. You're too important to each other. Have you tried to contact her?"

"Nope."

The foreman's responding chuckle lacked any humor. "With all the women you've dated, I figured for sure you understood them."

Nick's lips twisted in a poor parody of a smile. "What man has ever truly understood a woman?"

Palmer thumped his chest with his thumb. "You're looking at one. Why do you think my marriage has lasted twenty years and counting? If you miss Dani, do something about it."

She wouldn't want to see him. "She probably won't talk to me."

The foreman gaped at him as if his brain had fallen out of his head. "When someone is that important to you, you don't take no for an answer."

Dani *was* important to Nick, but he didn't want to make things even worse for her.

She was better off without him.

Besides, he needed to stay focused on moving the ranch further into the black.

He spent Sunday by himself, doing just that—checking through price lists for new cattle to replace those he'd sold, making a new budget that accommodated the money he'd made, washing the truck. And keeping his mind off Dani.

It was best that way. So why was he miserable?

FRIDAY AT THREE O'CLOCK, Nick entered the courthouse to witness his mother's third wedding. As she'd promised, the affair was small and simple, with the entire ceremony lasting roughly a quarter of an hour. Afterward, the happy couple treated Nick, Jamie and Hank to an early dinner at a restaurant near the courthouse. It was a beautiful afternoon, warm and sunny, with a light breeze.

Nick's mother looked radiant. Dave seemed pretty darned happy, too. They'd been together long enough to know each other's quirks and habits. And totally out of character, his mother had agreed to a small, inexpensive wedding instead of a big, costly one. Maybe this marriage would actually stick.

To help celebrate the joyous occasion, the restaurant sat them at a table festooned with flowers and gave them a free bottle of champagne. A few glasses of bubbly, and the joyous mood rose to new heights.

For everyone except Nick.

When Dave cracked a joke and Nick glared rather than laugh, his sister elbowed him hard.

"Ow!" He trained his glare on her. "What'd you do that for?"

"This marriage is a wonderful thing for both Mom and Dave. At least pretend you're happy for them," she chided.

"I *am* happy for them."

"If this is your definition of happy, I'd hate to see you miserable."

Nick excused himself to get some air and use the facilities. When he exited the men's room, his mother was waiting for him.

She took his arm and steered him to a bench under a loft tree outside. "Son, are you all right?"

"Yeah." He wanted to punch something, but he couldn't have said why. Instead, he shoved his hands in his pants pockets.

"Well, you look terrible. That chip on your shoulder doesn't suit you at all. It's this trouble with Dani, isn't it?"

Having nothing to say about that, he frowned at a flower, bowing in the soft wind.

"She's the best thing to ever happen to you, and yet you let her walk out of your life?" His mother made a disgusted sound. "You can be awfully thick-headed."

"I'm so glad I came today," he muttered.

His mother scrutinized him. "I swear, there are times you remind me so much of your father."

"What's that supposed to mean?"

"You don't smile, you don't make conversation. You're spoiling for a fight. That black cloud over your head won't do you or anyone else any good."

"What black cloud? And you and I both know that Dad had a solid reason to be bitter."

"I hurt him, and I'm sorry for that and for what I did." His mother bit her lip and appeared contrite. "And I'm grateful that at the end, he forgave me. But the breakup of our marriage wasn't all my fault."

Nick snickered. "The hell it wasn't."

She opened her mouth, seemed to hesitate, then sighed. "It's time you knew the full story."

Her excuses for cheating were the last thing Nick wanted to hear, but she really wanted to talk. He shrugged. "I can't wait to hear this."

"Thank you." Looking relieved, she went on. "Your father and I never talked much about our feelings, but before we got married, I made sure he understood that I was independent and that I needed more than just the ranch and kids to be happy. I wanted close female friends and a career. He led me to believe that he supported me in that, but I quickly found out that he didn't. He wanted to be my everything, so that I wouldn't want other people in my life or a career. When he realized that he couldn't possibly do that, he tried to buy my happiness with things."

Nick opened his mouth to remind her that she'd sure never complained about the jewelry and fancy clothes he lavished on her, but she wouldn't let him speak.

"It's true that I love beautiful things, Nick, but what your father did wasn't love. It was control. It was his need to control my life that destroyed our marriage and cost us the ranch."

With her words, some of the puzzling things Nick had never understood fell into place. His father, despondent and brooding for days on end for no seeming reason, the arguments between his parents that had started long before they'd sold the ranch. His mother's unhappiness despite the expensive gifts from his father. None of it had ever quite added up.

Now it did. He'd always blamed his mother for the loss of the ranch and the divorce, but he realized now that a fair portion of the blame lay with his father.

"Why did you let me believe everything that happened was your fault?" he asked.

"Guilt. I started up with another man while I was still married to your father, and that was wrong. But this isn't about what I did or your father's control issues. It isn't about his bitterness, either—it's about your own. Don't be like him. Don't let it eat you alive."

Startled at the words, Nick frowned. "I'm not bitter."

"Oh, no? The next time you glance in the mirror, take a good look at yourself."

The rest of the day and into the night, he chewed over his mother's advice. He didn't want to be like his father, had always prided himself on being upbeat and content with his life.

Sure, he was out of sorts right now and maybe a little angry, but he wasn't bitter.

Was he?

He thought back on his behavior over the past several weeks. Sometime in the wee hours, he realized that his mother was dead on. Without Dani in his life, he'd become hostile, unfriendly and negative—just as his father had been the last eighteen years of his life. Yes, he'd managed to save the ranch, but he wasn't any happier than his father had been.

Mad at himself for slipping into such a dark place, Nick flipped on the reading lamp. Blinking in the harsh light, he sat up. "What the hell am I going to do?" he wondered out loud.

He didn't have to think long before the answer came to him. For starters, he was going to kick his bitterness on its ass and right out of his life.

Yeah, that felt pretty good.

Next he considered his father's need to control his mother. That disgusted him, and caused him to look at both his parents from a different perspective. Neither of them was more responsible than the other for their financial problems or their failed marriage. That was a real eye-opener. If only they'd talked to each other about their feelings...but they hadn't.

Nick was thankful that he didn't share the urge to control other people. He was grateful, too, that he and Dani had always been able to talk to each other about anything and everything.

Great.

So now what?

In the silence, Palmer's words echoed in his mind. *When someone is that important to you, you don't take no for an answer.*

Dani was more than important. She was everything.

In a flash, everything came clear. He was in love with her.

Nick swallowed hard, but there was no use denying it. He loved Dani.

Admitting that scared the hell out of him, but living the rest of his life without her scared him more.

Loving her wouldn't distract him from focusing on making the ranch profitable, it would help. She wanted marriage and kids. Shock of all shocks, Nick realized that he did, too. He hadn't wanted to repeat his parents' patterns, but he realized now that he never would.

Suddenly he knew exactly what to do.

SHORTLY AFTER BIG MAMA'S CAFÉ unlocked its doors for the grand reopening Saturday morning, Nick entered the restaurant. The place was packed with people, some of whom he recognized. Lots of new faces, too, which was a definite positive.

Dani was sure to be busy, but this couldn't wait.

Naomi was showing someone to a table, leaving the hostess station empty. Beside it, Big Mama sat on a high chair. Nick hadn't seen or spoken with her since his split with Dani. She stared coolly at him without so much as a twitch of her lips. That stung, but he deserved it for being a jackass.

Determined to make amends, he greeted her. "You're looking like your regular self again, Big Mama, but shouldn't you be at home, recuperating?" he asked over the noise.

Some of the stiffness eased from her posture. "The doctor cleared me for a few hours. It's nice to see you, Nick. You look good yourself. Maybe a little tired. I don't believe you've been this dressed up since you and Dani double-dated to your senior prom."

He was wearing a sports coat and dress pants because what he wanted to say to Dani was important.

"Dani's done a wonderful job with the remodel, hasn't she? The skylight and our pretty wheat-colored walls make the restaurant so bright and cheerful, and our beautiful ceramic light fixtures really add to the ambiance."

Nick glanced up, then around, past the sea of people and nodded absently. "Where is she?"

Big Mama gave him an astute once-over, and at last smiled. "It's crazy today. I haven't seen her since we unlocked the doors, but she's around here somewhere."

"Thanks. Talk to you later."

He turned around and ran smack into Sly, Lana and their cute little girl. Sly about scowled him to death.

Nick ignored the other man's dirty glare. "Can you point me in Dani's direction?" he asked.

"She's busy."

"I need to find her."

"What for? You broke her heart."

"Hush, Sly," Lana said, placing her hand on the big rancher's forearm.

He let out a painstaking sigh. "What do you want with her?"

"That's private," Nick said. "But it's all good."

Provided he could convince Dani to forgive him for being such a lunkhead.

A long look passed between him and Sly before Sly nodded. "When I last saw her, she was headed for the kitchen."

Nick was on his way there when the door swung open and Dani headed through it. Her hair was tied back, and she was dressed in a short, bright spring dress. It was obvious she loved the excitement—her face was flushed and her eyes sparkled. She'd never looked so beautiful.

Warmth filled Nick's chest. "Hey," he said, moving toward her.

"Nick." Her eyes widened and her eyebrows jumped in surprise. "I— You— Um, you're here."

"That's right. The place looks great. I want to talk to you."

"Now? Have you noticed the size of this crowd? We're swamped, and even with Sadie, Colleen and Melanie waitressing, I need to pitch in and help. I don't have time."

"Make time. People will understand."

He grabbed her hand and pulled her forward. Dani dug in her heels. "You haven't called me in over a month," she said. "You can't just waltz in here and expect me to go blindly off with you to talk."

Nick couldn't believe he'd waited so long. He wanted badly to make up for the lost weeks. "I have important things to say to you."

"They'll have to wait," she said firmly.

This was a side of Dani he didn't recognize. "There's something different about you."

"I put myself first now and do what I want to do," she said. "At the moment, I want to make sure all these customers are happy so that they come back often. Excuse me."

Nick put two fingers in his mouth and whistled. Instantly the room quieted.

"Dani, I have something to say to you," he announced. "If this is the only way you'll listen, so be it."

Regulars and new faces were all staring avidly at them. Nick spotted Palmer and his wife across the way. The foreman gave him a thumbs-up and a grin.

Dani rolled her eyes. "Go on and talk then, so I can get to work again."

At a nearby table, Janelle, Becca, Christy and Per watched wide-eyed, making Nick feel like a specimen in a glass fish bowl.

Damn. He'd meant this to be private. He cleared his throat. "This past few months, I've— Hell, I can't do this here. Dani's taking a short break." He grabbed hold of her elbow.

"I can't leave right now," she repeated, again digging in her heels.

"We'll be fine," someone assured her.

"You two go on and patch things up." That was Jewel, and she was smiling like somebody's doting grandma.

Nick steered Dani through the doors that led to the office.

As soon as they stepped into the room, he closed and locked the door, shutting out the noise.

"About what I was saying," he continued. "Remember when your mom was in the hospital and we talked about my father's heart attack? We both wanted our parents to make appointments their doctors, but neither of them listened to us. I realized then that I can't make anyone do what they don't want to do. That's a long way of saying that I can't make you forgive me for hurting you, but I'm sure as hell going to try."

The skeptical lift of her eyebrows wasn't exactly encouraging, but Nick wasn't about to let that stop him.

"This past month, I've missed you," he said.

"Could've fooled me."

Her arms were crossed now, and she still wore that doubtful expression. She wasn't making this easy.

"I was trying to give us both space," he explained.

"Right." She compressed her lips.

"It's true."

"I really don't want to hear about—"

"Will you please just listen."

Dani glanced at the ceiling and sighed, but she kept her mouth closed.

"I realize that I don't want space. And I've learned something that I think you'll want to hear. Without you, my life is empty. *I'm* empty."

He had her attention now. She angled her chin a fraction. "Go on."

Nick took that as a positive sign. This next part almost stuck in his throat, but he needed to say it. "I've been a stubborn fool. Dani Pettit, I love you. I think I always have, but I've been too pig-headed and scared to admit it."

Later he would tell her what he'd learned from his mother and how the new insights had changed him. "That's why no other woman has ever held my interest for long."

"You loved Ashley."

"The woman I met in college?" Nick scoffed. "At the time I assumed I did, but compared to my feelings for you, she was just a crush. I love how independent you are. I love your big heart and your enthusiasm and your mac and cheese casserole. You're not afraid to stand up to me, either, and I love that. I don't care much for those chick flicks you make me watch, but they make you happy, and that's what matters." He shut his mouth.

Dani just stood there, staring at him. He couldn't read her expression. "Say something," he urged.

"I'm dumbfounded."

Not what he'd hoped to hear. With a sinking feeling, Nick realized he'd waited too long to talk to her. Still, he had to try. "Just tell me the truth," he said. "Have I lost my chance with you?"

For a long moment she let the question dangle in the air.

He was about to go crazy when she shook her head.

"You think I'm that fickle? Well, think again. Because I love you, too."

Relief almost bowled him over. "Come here, you."

He pulled her into his arms and kissed her soundly. Holding her again was like coming home. When they were both breathing hard, he broke away and rested his forehead against hers. "What's your stance on getting married?"

"You already know the answer to that—someday I definitely will."

"I mean to me. Now."

She pushed him away and made a face. "Marriage isn't for you—you've always said so."

"Hey, a guy can change his mind. I've let go of the past and it doesn't scare me anymore. I love you, Dani, and I never want you out of my life again. How about it?"

She re-crossed her arms. "I want kids."

Nick pictured a couple of little Danis, running around the ranch. "You drive a hard bargain, woman. Lucky for you, so do I."

He went down on one knee and clasped her hands. "Dani, I love you, and I promise to do everything in my power to make you happy now and forever. Put me out of my misery and marry me. The sooner, the better."

Her eyes filled. "Yes, Nick, I'll marry you."

Outside the door, people cheered.

Nosy so and so's, but Nick was too busy kissing the woman he loved to care.

* * * * *

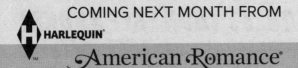

COMING NEXT MONTH FROM

HARLEQUIN®

American Romance®

Available November 4, 2014

REQUEST YOUR FREE BOOKS!
2 FREE NOVELS PLUS 2 FREE GIFTS!

⊞HARLEQUIN®

American ★ Romance®

LOVE, HOME & HAPPINESS

YES! Please send me 2 FREE Harlequin® American Romance® novels and my 2 FREE gifts (gifts are worth about $10). After receiving them, if I don't wish to receive any more books, I can return the shipping statement marked "cancel." If I don't cancel, I will receive 4 brand-new novels every month and be billed just $4.74 per book in the U.S. or $5.24 per book in Canada. That's a savings of at least 14% off the cover price! It's quite a bargain! Shipping and handling is just 50¢ per book in the U.S. and 75¢ per book in Canada.* I understand that accepting the 2 free books and gifts places me under no obligation to buy anything. I can always return a shipment and cancel at any time. Even if I never buy another book, the two free books and gifts are mine to keep forever.

154/354 HDN F4YN

Name _____ (PLEASE PRINT) _____

Address _____ Apt. # _____

City _____ State/Prov. _____ Zip/Postal Code _____

Signature (if under 18, a parent or guardian must sign)

Mail to the **Harlequin® Reader Service:**
IN U.S.A.: P.O. Box 1867, Buffalo, NY 14240-1867
IN CANADA: P.O. Box 609, Fort Erie, Ontario L2A 5X3

Want to try two free books from another line?
Call 1-800-873-8635 or visit www.ReaderService.com.

* Terms and prices subject to change without notice. Prices do not include applicable taxes. Sales tax applicable in N.Y. Canadian residents will be charged applicable taxes. Offer not valid in Quebec. This offer is limited to one order per household. Not valid for current subscribers to Harlequin American Romance books. All orders subject to credit approval. Credit or debit balances in a customer's account(s) may be offset by any other outstanding balance owed by or to the customer. Please allow 4 to 6 weeks for delivery. Offer available while quantities last.

Your Privacy—The Harlequin® Reader Service is committed to protecting your privacy. Our Privacy Policy is available online at www.ReaderService.com or upon request from the Harlequin Reader Service.

We make a portion of our mailing list available to reputable third parties that offer products we believe may interest you. If you prefer that we not exchange your name with third parties, or if you wish to clarify or modify your communication preferences, please visit us at www.ReaderService.com/consumerchoice or write to us at Harlequin Reader Service Preference Service, P.O. Box 9062, Buffalo, NY 14269. Include your complete name and address.

HARI3R

SPECIAL EXCERPT FROM

HARLEQUIN®

American Romance®

Read on for a sneak peek of
THE SEAL'S HOLIDAY BABIES
by USA TODAY *bestselling author Tina Leonard!*

"Don't you have anything to say for yourself?" Jade demanded.

"I'm content to let you do all the talking." Ty settled himself comfortably, watching her face.

She sat next to him so she could look closely at him to press her case, he supposed, but the shock of her so close to him—almost in his space—was enough to brain-wipe what little sense he had in his head. She smelled good, like spring flowers breaking through a long, cold winter. He shook his head to clear the sudden madness diluting his gray matter. "You're beautiful," he said, the words popping out before he could put on the Dumbass Brake.

The Dumbass Brake had saved him many a time, but today, it seemed to have gotten stuck.

"What?" Jade said. Her mesmerizing green eyes stared at him, stunned.

He was half drowning, might as well go for full immersion. "You're beautiful," he repeated.

She looked at him for a long moment, then scoffed. "Ty Spurlock, don't you dare try to sweet-talk me. If there's one thing I know about you, it's that sugar flows out of your mouth like a river of honey when you're making a mess. The bigger the jam, the sweeter and deeper the talk." She got up, and Ty cursed the disappearance of the brake that had deserted him just when he'd needed it most.

He smelled that sweet perfume again, was riveted by the soft red sweater covering delicate breasts. "Okay, fine. Everything is fine."

"It's not fine yet." She smiled, leaned over and gave him a long, sweet, not-sisterly-at-all smooch on the lips. Shocked, he sat still as a concrete gargoyle, frozen and immobilized, too scared to move and scare her off.

She pulled away far too soon. "*Now* it's fine."

Indeed it was. He couldn't stop staring at the mouth that had worked such magic on him, stolen his breath, stolen his heart. He gazed into her eyes, completely lost in the script.

"What was that for?"

Jade got up, went to the door and opened it. Cold air rushed in, and a supersize sheet of snow fell from the overhang, but he couldn't take his eyes off her.

"Because I felt like it," Jade said, then left.

Look For
THE SEAL'S HOLIDAY BABIES
by TINA LEONARD
*Part of the **BRIDESMAIDS CREEK** miniseries*
from Harlequin® American Romance®.

Available November 2014
wherever books and ebooks are sold.

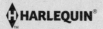

American Romance®

Returning to Crooked Valley is to ex-soldier Duke Duggan more terrifying than the battlefield. Still, Duke has only one reason to be back—taking control of his late grandfather's ranch. But being thrown headfirst into ranch life sees Duke like a fish out of water.

That is until he sees Carrie Coulter again. He may be steadfastly proud, but Carrie has learned never to take no for an answer—especially from a cowboy crying out for her expertise.

As Christmas approaches they finally let the magic of the season sweep them away!

Look for
The Cowboy's Christmas Gift
by DONNA ALWARD

Part of the *Crooked Valley Ranch* miniseries from Harlequin® American Romance®.

Available November 2014 wherever books and ebooks are sold.

HAR75543

HARLEQUIN®

A *Romance* FOR EVERY MOOD™

Love the Harlequin book you just read?

Your opinion matters.

Review this book on your favorite
book site, review site, blog or your own
social media properties and share
your opinion with other readers!